T0279498

The Javelin Thrower

THE ITALIAN LIST

PAOLO VOLPONI

The Javelin Thrower

WITH AN AFTERWORD BY EMANUELE ZINATO

TRANSLATED BY RICHARD DIXON

LONDON   NEW YORK   CALCUTTA

SERIES EDITOR
Alberto Toscano

Seagull Books, 2018

Originally published as Paolo Volponi, Il lanciatore di giavellotto.
© Giulio Einaudi editore s.p.a., Turin, 1981

Afterword by Emanuele Zinato
© Giulio Einaudi editore s.p.a., Turin, 2015

First published in English translation by Seagull Books, 2018

English translation © Richard Dixon, 2018

ISBN   978 0 8574 2 539 3

British Library Cataloguing-in-Publication Data
A catalogue record for this book is available from the British Library

Typeset by Seagull Books, Calcutta, India
Printed and bound by Hyam Enterprises, Calcutta, India

CONTENTS

The Javelin Thrower

I

Family Garden. The Great Screens.
Maternal Possession

FROM MID-OCTOBER, with the morning gleaming whiter against the window and the noise of the river reaching inside the house, the cloud and the fig tree became fixed points for Damiano Possanza. As he prepared for the new day, all that held his sight and mind was the greyish coil that obscured the sun and the green stain of the tree.

The cloud had sat still over the river for several days, at the same height, always the same shape and colour until sunset, when it burst into flame; and in the evening it died down to an ashen white. Even at night the cloud pressed in on the river gorge, between the dark slopes of the mountains.

By dawn the fig tree could already be seen outstretched, half-green and half-yellow across the outside wall, contrasting with the hillside and the edge of the cloud on the other side of the river. The effect of the two shades of leaf seemed to produce a continual superimposition of one upon the other.

Possanza had done well in his choice of a Sultane-fig sapling, and the ground in which it grew, and the breezes to which it was entrusted. He had planted it there to mark the birth of his first grandson who by family tradition would take his name, and as the fig flourished it would accompany the boy as he grew.

Young Damiano and the fig tree had now reached the age of nine, and both were in good health. The school year had just begun, and he would set off each day before his grandfather, after stopping to watch him for a moment shaving at the window with his cut-throat razor, badger brush and bowl brimful of almond-scented foam. To bid goodbye he would touch the belt that hung open at either side of his waist, and would then close the front door behind him with a manly slam rather than holding it by the latch.

The cloud floated and its reflection licked against the stair rail.

The fig tree continued its game of tag with its various branches, window by window. The kitchen window was half-open and Possanza's daughter-in-law stood before it, illuminated by its light, wearing a fancy pink dressing gown. Her awkward banging of dishes at the sink rang out one after the other with a strange persistency, like a call or a song.

Possanza tried not to gaze at that pretty half-dressed woman, whose neck and arms were completely bare, whose breasts swayed beneath her shiny nightdress. He went across to look at Lavinia, his young granddaughter, who was still in her cot at the foot of her parents' bed. But as well as the comforting tenderness of her sleep he caught sight, whether voluntarily or not he couldn't say, of the unmade bed pulled down on the wife's side, and he noted a fragrance that would stay with him for some while, until it later melded with the touch of the clay as he worked it.

The house, modernized less than ten years before, in preparation for his son's wedding, was small, hardly enough to contain the family.

At night his bedroom wall came to life with the noises from the next room, noises that he was obliged to piece together into a story full of pictures and blanks, that altered in a manner ever more insistent. He was tantalized even by the silence, by its heaviness and its duration.

The decision to build a single outside wash house had been a great mistake; it was now filled with a jumble of garments, soaps and scent bottles whose significance he could no longer comprehend or put into any order. It had been his practice for some time to use the wash house only in the evening or at midday when the others were least likely to be around. But his daughter-in-law had now taken to shutting herself in there last thing at night.

POSSANZA LEFT THAT MORNING without even taking coffee, so as not to go into the kitchen, close to the young woman, and he set off towards the pottery thinking about the new pots he had to prepare. He focused on the image of smaller plates, with a cloud at the centre, each like a patch of the autumn sky that accompanied him, dull but clear; the vases and cooking pots, edged with fig leaves whose fragrance he could almost smell. He was a master craftsman, almost an artist, and as such he had to make a living and fend for himself.

Even the great Adolfo De Carolis had praised his pottery at Pesaro in 1918 and had bought a number of his pots, preferring them to those in majolica from the more artistic workshops run by academy teachers. And the following year he had sent him a letter of compliments and an issue of the journal *La Fionda* in which he had published an article about popular art, referring to him when he wrote that all modern decoration ought to return to the search for 'a childlike freshness and truth'.

Possanza had responded by sending the master, by way of his son when he arrived in Milan on his honeymoon, two thirty-centimetre dishes, the vertical sides of which were completely dove-grey, with terracotta lines brushed across the centre, and in the middle a bunch of black grapes tied to two yellow corncobs. Maestro De Carolis had sent his compliments once again and in return had given him a woodcut self-portrait of 1904 in which he appeared dressed as an artist against a printed page, the copy being signed and dated May 1919, dedicated to the noblest of all Marche and Umbrian master potters.

This should have given a new feeling of youth and determination to Possanza, now fifty-eight, and the owner of a pottery works, the adjoining clay pit on the right lower bank of the river Metauro, and the farm and cottage connected to it by a four-hectare field, with a small vineyard and an orchard of apples, walnuts, cherries and pomegranates. These now produced little fruit but had plenty of boughs and trunks of sweet-smelling timber, suitable for more delicate kiln firings.

He came across his wife and stopped her, though he had nothing to say. She was no longer beautiful: the thick mane of sandy-blond hair pinned up from her neck had lost its colour; her face had now broadened out, while the more feminine parts of her body had withered. Her arms and legs were now knobbly and her buttocks had sagged. She had no children, and this was also why she had increased her sessions of prayer. When Damiano went on top of her in bed, all she could do was sigh and respond as though it were a duty, and while he lifted her nightdress from below, she would fasten it at the top. He had married her at the end of the second year of the war, as soon as his son had gone to join the army. By that time he had been a widower for over fifteen years. It was difficult even then to get much conversation out of her; but her body was as plump and pliant as a chestnut, and at the same time sweet and nourishing. She had come from the country-side but had been employed by Count Trapassi's family since she was a young girl, at their house on the main square whose front door was next to the windows of the main tavern. Through those windows he had watched and nurtured a desire for her, blurring the clear image of the maid into the glow and aroma of his glass of hot anisette.

He made love to her only rarely now, when he could no longer resist the sounds from the next room. He no longer knew how to talk to her as a husband, especially in the company of others, at mealtimes or after supper. His love for his wife had faded just like her blond hair; but Damiano hadn't yet questioned to how much it had been rekindled in the rich colours of his daughter-in-law. He had to carry on regardless; or he concentrated on the problems and complications of work, which he himself created and complicated. But even sitting at the potter's wheel, certain scents and colours returned and remained, as though inside the clay he was handling.

THE CLAY AND THE EQUIPMENT had been prepared for him by his son Dorino, who was kneeling at the far end of the yard painting a standard series of jars ready for firing. He looked at himself long and hard in the mirror he kept beside the largest wheel for making measurements and comparing other objects and models; he decided to continue with the idea of painting the cloud and the fig tree: the countless yellow-green leaves as thick as plumage. He tied his scarf around his neck in the way he had done throughout his adult life, pinning the knot with a Roman cameo he had found in the clay pit, and set to work on the first plate.

His hands found their way into the indulgent clay as new scents and ideas mixed with those already there and lingering: he added water or slip and kneaded the clay following his own mastery, detached from his hands and from his thoughts. He realized he was hesitating to give it form; he was still handling and turning the clay not knowing what object to make.

He left the wheel and went to get the colours, the slivers of ochre and chalk that he mixed between his fingers, making haloes of new colour. They seemed infinite over the edge of the wheel. Looking at them he felt sure he would lose himself behind their continual flexibility and realized that the cloud and the fig tree were two great screens drawn over the oppressive truth, screens he himself operated, as did the whole world. He chose the clays and the bowls of kaolin one by one with no clear plan, arranging them carefully as if the order in which they were arranged might also provide him with some answer. He took the clay and threw two cooking pots, then two larger ones; he was searching for the tone of sound that his daughter-in-law had sent out from the kitchen. But he was uncertain there as well, and started trying to form the shape of a vase that was all neck, with a slender mouth at the top.

Young Damiano opened his exercise book in the middle of the dinner plates to show his grandfather the triangles and circles he had been drawing at school for the first time with a pair of compasses and ink, to prove a geometrical theory. Those shapes, drawn and measured, seemed very like the work of a craftsman. The table shook and clattered under his proud force. His mother was there beside him, laying out the napkins.

'Damiano,' she said, 'this isn't the right time. Your granddad has to eat now, and so do we, and your exercise book might get dirty.'

'Let him be. I can see Damìn's excited.'

Damìn was the nickname Damiano used for his grandson so that he wouldn't hear his own name being used for anyone else. It was family tradition that when he died his grandson would then be called Damiano, or when the boy reached adulthood. He himself had been called Damìn till the age of thirteen.

'Damìn wants to show us how clever he is, like all the Possanza family. This homework's important—it's an important day for him.'

'He's not bothering you? Aren't you tired?' his daughter-in-law asked.

'Tired. From what? I've worked less than usual today. It's Damìn who's done the work, working for his grandfather too, and you want to stop him showing us his homework. Move the plates aside. Let Damìn have all the space he needs to show us how clever he is. Come and see, you first, as you're his mother.'

Damìn looked up from his exercise book and beamed at his grandfather and his mother. He felt a great satisfaction whenever these two adults were together, even by chance or in passing. That was what he waited for each day and what crowned his boundless admiration for his grandfather and his loving sense of possession towards his mother. Damìn also adored his grandmother, with a clear feeling he could experience whenever and however he wished, as soon as that feeling arose, with a hug or a childish prank. He also felt a golden and uncomplicated sense of possession towards his sister Lavinia, beyond that soft and enveloping blanket in which he and his mother were wrapped, larger than them and their entire world.

Sleep also had the same warm and boundless texture; and fleeting moments of awareness from his earliest childhood still floated there. Ever recurrent was that flushed waking to take his milk, to throw himself on the warm wave of his mother's body. His sister, whom he called Vitina for short, as well for affection, belonged to him to the extent that he could lift her up and move her about as he wished, or could cover her with his body and kiss her, or make her cry or laugh, pinch her or hug her, lick her or bite her, lead her around the house or close her up in a corner—always in the same place, behind the door in the passageway, under the coats and the scarves, where their father's shoes lay alone. Those shoes were an impenetrable and hostile element in his world: they opened up a space that was measureless, but that tended to fall, to recede over so many surfaces and gaps, like the shadow of the shutters on the front wall. He could never properly understand where his father was and what he was made of—not even when his father was sitting in front of him at table. There was always something about him and his manner that escaped him, becoming like a sharp line or a heavy ray of light that struck him as it fell.

The centre of his world was the figure of his grandfather, which grew larger and brighter every day. He was strong and tall, malleable, and also useful for better enjoying and exercising his feeling of possession over his mother.

The recurring joy that sustained him in all and everything was his memory of clutching his mother's breast, with one hand thrust between her bosom and the other stretched out to touch his grandfather's face: his mouth and his moustache.

Damìn's father wasn't part of that picture in which truth was built and promoted by familiar figures and voices. So that he never heard his father's voice welling and remaining within him; but it seemed to him each time to be something external and new, coming from some other place.

PLEASED WITH THE EXCHANGE between his mother and his grandfather, Damìn put his exercise book away and lifted his sister onto her chair. He handed her silver fork and spoon to her and brushed back her pigtails. He went to wash his hands at the basin in which his grandfather had just washed, then took his place at table, opposite the head of the family.

In front of him was the glazed terracotta cup his grandfather had made especially for him, with a fox and a raven painted around it, looking at each other laughing and snarling. The fox and the raven had become a part of his real world and had their own ever-present voices that spoke to him, full of cunning and empty promises.

'What have you started work on?' Dorino asked his father.

'Not sure yet. A series of pictorial plates . . . some glazed vases . . . '

'They'll be nice, I'm sure . . . But for the winter we need two or three loads of jugs and cooking pots . . . ordinary, saleable—and some braziers and hotplates of various sizes as well.'

'Don't you talk about these things at work?' asked Norma.

'Not much,' answered Damiano. 'We have different jobs in different places. Like you and my wife here at home.'

'Your wife has little to say, she's busy praying.'

'Well I have to pray as well.'

'And who do you pray to?'

'The patron saint of potters, the protector of ceramics . . . the guardian of time . . . Pots are full of time . . . The soul of the earth, of colours.'

'You're praying to those who can't hear and have no need of it,' said Grandma sweetly.

'And if they turn against me . . . the clay, the stones, the fire, the slip? They too require much prayer, much love. More than the souls in your purgatory.'

'But no one turns against you—nothing and no one,' said Norma again, and her son repeated her words in his mind.

'I'll start turning against someone if you don't help me with production,' declared Dorino. 'You've got to help me choose durable clays, those that fire easily ... preferably with a colour, though just a hint.'

'But a pot of the kind you want isn't coloured. You, for example ... what colour could I paint you? I could paint Damìn, or Vitina ...' and it was hard to hold him back, so that Damìn felt free to carry on.

'Mama ...'

'Mama? And what colour do you want to paint your mother?'

'Purple, I'd do her in purple, with a light-blue handle ... and with a red, shiny mouth ...'

'But then you'd have to keep a Mama like that all for yourself—a purple Mama with a red handle.'

Damìn laughed with glee.

'You really have to give me a hand. Or we'll make less this year than last, and we'll lose customers. And if people start buying pans made of tin, then no one's ever going to stop them.'

'Yes. But what woman is going to cook using aluminium? Everything's tasteless ... everything's the same, cooked in the same way. And the fire always has to be hotter, until it catches and burns. Who can afford to be so wasteful with fire? Terracotta absorbs, keeps the heat. Try cooking kidney beans in aluminium! Or polenta

15

or fish! And people don't worry just about the taste, but the appearance. You have two men working for you.'

'But you're the best.'

'And so? My plates and vases will also be sold.'

'Yes, of course. They're very nice. But few of them sell . . . and not at the fair, not directly by us. You could give them to the shops, but for how much, and when do they actually pay you? How many get broken and stolen by that time? Soon there'll be our six-monthly payment on the mortgage. Do you have the money for that?'

'No. But soon, as you say, soon . . . it'll be Christmas. What's making you so low today? I can just as well delay the instalment, ask for credit.'

'We have half the money and could make the rest at one fair alone, or with two or three wholesalers along the via Flaminia. That's why I say we must set to work producing. With our reputation, we could sell pots even without firing them. Our real problem is output and a truck to go and sell them.'

'Who would you send off with a truck? Damìn? His mother?'

Damìn happily followed the conversation, keeping a constant eye on his grandfather and his mother who together seemed jubilant.

'You're an artist. You go and shut yourself away . . . with your masterpieces. I want to set up an industrial concern, with our name and our vehicles, and government help.'

'Mussolini's government? You'd throw yourself behind that lot? Industry has killed off the families of the master potters, even the kiln workers . . . in Pergola, San Lorenzo, Urbino, Orciano. Those who get rich have sold out, the servants of Fascism—even if they manufacture urinals . . . and much more of what goes into them. I'm not getting involved with Fascist industry, not me. Our ancestors have been putting our name on every pot for the past two hundred years, even the most ordinary ones, those simply glazed around the mouth . . . D.P. interwoven . . . or they'd design a mint leaf, with a hint of green that flavoured even the water, or on our cooking pots, a small garlic, a tomato, a chickpea, depending on the size. Rotilanti, the lawyer in Urbino, still collects them: he'll pay as much as twenty lire a piece if he finds one, prizes them more than real majolica—and Rotilanti knows what he's talking about, he's a gentleman. When the King went through Urbino in 1909, he wore mourning for a month and went a whole week without talking to anyone. "Possanza," he told me last time, "carry on, Possanza, you carry on . . . and there'll still be some hope for this wretched country." And so, I say, both of us don't have to continue doing exactly the same thing! You follow your own ideas if you want to. You're hardworking and you're a good salesman as well. Perhaps you're not a master potter. You've taken after your mother's side of the family more than the Possanzas—you're more of a tradesman, a man of ideas. You can't spend a day at the wheel like I do, or a day in the yard. You're drawn more by the fairs and the banks than by the clay.'

His daughter-in-law and grandson gave him looks of full support.

'Damìn's right,' he continued. 'Each of us is made with a different-coloured handle and a different-coloured mouth. And I don't want to knock your handle, nor even less to mix the colour of your mouth. It's difficult enough interweaving the D with the P on the edge of the plate . . . and then again the colours don't hold so well today. I'll still help you out for the whole of the new year and beyond—jars and pans, all lined up like ears of corn in a field. But then, that's it. You carry on with your commercial production and I'll do mine—you with your ideas about industry and me with my pots . . . '

Damìn was listening intently to his grandfather and didn't suppose for a moment that his father would contradict a single word: though his father's word would have meant little, even if he were in agreement. Damìn got down from his chair and went to his mother, still watching his grandfather. As he followed his gestures, he traced his hand over an apple on his mother's plate.

Damiano Possanza, sapped by bitterness at his son's frequent opposition, followed that hand and stared at the green colour of the apple, gentle but firm. Another shade of colour that caught his eye was the satin-pink dress of the young woman sitting at the table.

II

The Silver Dagger. The Scene and the Reality.
The Love of Women

BY THE END OF THE WINTER, Possanza had satisfied his son's production requirements and managed to work on a series of his own pieces: he was eagerly working to complete several orders but still felt pressed by another more important urge that hung over him each day and over his whole life, an urge already present and definable but which he had not yet decided whether to realize. He held on to it like a dream that might itself become a source of happiness, against which he had to measure and better himself. A large vase began to take form in his head, beautiful and delicate, in shades of colour that altered with the changing seasons.

Easter fell on 19th April, the day of Lavinia's sixth birthday, and to celebrate the happy coincidence the family took a trip on Easter Monday up Monte Petrano.

The wide mountain plateau was not yet in flower, but its soft mantle of new grass was filled with an infinity of restless insects, small green grasshoppers in particular, which could jump higher than a man and would rise in swarms weaving an immense sail in the air.

After lunch on the grass, Damiano and his grandson moved away from the group, looking for the first daffodils. They wandered about for a long time, kneeling down every so often below the suspended flight of a skylark who seemed to be waiting to answer some human call. Damìn couldn't manage to imitate that sound and was then annoyed by the birds that came to hover closer by.

When it was time to go back they followed a series of hillocks dotted alongside coppices of dogwood and beech. Suddenly behind one of these shrubs they glimpsed Damìn's mother, her hair loose, bent down naked to relieve herself. They were both caught by surprise, both deeply struck by a sense of embarrassment and shock. It was Damìn who openly gestured to his grandfather to keep quiet and be still, pointing to his mother's naked back. He remained transfixed, his hand raised, not revealing his presence nor moving on, smiling to keep his courage.

But an awareness that he couldn't fully satisfy his enjoyment prompted him to turn once more to his grandfather. Only through him could he intensify the pleasure of that sight and enjoy the pleasure aroused by their complicity.

The woman stood up and after wiping herself dry she dressed again and headed off in the opposite direction. Damìn smiled broadly, hardly containing his excitement; he took his grandfather's hand and led him to the point where she had been. Damiano followed his grandson but kept to the other side of the bush, neither speaking nor looking, breathing heavily. The grasshoppers and skylarks had vanished and the two now saw before them the mountain slopes stretching below—a great wide blue valley of crags that dropped gradually down to hills marked by fields and upland farmhouses. A great natural and living funnel that, for both of them, completed most appropriately the wonderful sight they had just seen.

THROUGHOUT THE AFTERNOON Damiano said almost nothing, and just before dusk he went off alone, leaving his grandson too. He lay down on the grass, completely still, with one saline thought that ran through his whole body.

Back home, he waited in the garden until the others had gone to bed and went to the wash house. He still dreaded finding some trace, any trace, of that body he had seen almost entirely naked, so much so that he stood staring at himself in the mirror, hardly breathing and with his mouth closed so as not to detect any odour. But he was quivering with desire. He took his cock in his right hand and pulled it up, into full view: it was swollen and blind in its determination. He gripped it more firmly, and felt a wave of pleasure and pride from it.

Once he had satisfied himself he remained in front of the mirror. His face bore the strain of his turmoil and instead of remorse he felt the urge to carry on, to stand before that woman's body that he continued to see. He searched more thoroughly among the items of clothing and among the soaps and scent bottles. He could find nothing direct, nor any reminder; the type of soap she used was still unopened inside its tissue wrapping.

He left the wash house and searched around the steps, in the kitchen, in the storeroom. He found nothing and his frustration grew. He went into the garden but there was no laundry hanging on the line, nor by the end of the house. Climbing up, on the top step he saw the outdoor shoes she had worn for their mountain trip, next to each other, unlaced: in two-tone suede, with a stitched toecap, the sole and flat heal made of natural rubber. He took them and hugged them; he clasped one in each hand, for a long time—he buried his face inside them and began kissing them, even the eyeholes, the laces. His head was filled with the slight fetor that came from them; little by little that odour drew him away from himself, from the possible truth of his own body and feeling, until he began to bathe them with his tears. He locked himself up again in the wash house, in front of the mirror, with her shoes tight against his neck and his cheeks. His hair and the bristles of his moustache fell between their creases and their soles, which grew more intimate the closer he inspected them. This lasted the whole night, until he was shaken by the crowing of cockerels from the river.

He put the shoes back and returned to the kitchen, in front of the window, waiting for the dawn light.

AT THE ELEVEN O'CLOCK MASS, standing beside his mother, Damìn could see that at the other end of the pew, in his smart uniform, was Traiano Marcacci, the head of the Fascists in Fossombrone, the man with the silver dagger. He swayed impudently, out of time with the chanting of the congregation, and gave Damìn's mother a sideways glance each time he reached the furthest point forward and the furthest back in his undulations.

The woman stared at her prayer book, but neither praying nor singing; she moved her lips as though she were mumbling something with ever-greater relish and guilt.

Damìn was seized by an almost furious anger when he read these feelings in her face and in her every movement. He saw Marcacci stretch out a hand towards his mother's book. She had instantly moved back her hands but the smirk on her lips was more pronounced.

Damìn had seen Marcacci on several previous Sundays, waiting by the cathedral door and then moving forward with the three of them towards the pews. He had kept closer to Vitina each time and some distance from their mother.

At the end of Mass, in the general eruption of relief, Marcacci had nodded to their mother and smiled, and had then bent right down to give Vitina a hug.

IN THE SECOND HALF OF MAY the feast-day Masses were packed together, one after the other, and Damìn's mother was anxious not to miss any of them, impatient to be there and busy in her preparations. Her hair was more resplendent than ever and caught the glances of the Fascist among the crowd. And her silks shone all the more beside the sashes of his military uniform. Beyond his white cotton gloves shone the silver buckle that held his taut black figure; beside it glinted his invincible dagger.

Damìn was pained by all the conjectures that overwhelmed him but could do nothing to hold them back, nor did he want to leave his place beside of his mother, before what was happening around her. One evening, during the benediction, he saw his mother's missal drop from her hands and Marcacci immediately pick it up.

She had rapidly leafed through it as if to clean it, blowing on it, but some trace must have remained, if only a folded page or a fingerprint over a word or just a letter. Damìn felt a burning urge to seize the book and had to grasp Vitina to keep control of himself. He didn't leave his sister until they were back home. Their mother went straight to her room and he led Vitina out into the garden before returning inside to spy through the keyhole: he saw the book on the dressing table and his mother pacing back and forth, looking into the mirror and tidying herself; he watched her sit on the bed, brush her hair repeatedly with just the same movement, and then gradually take off her clothes, pausing over each item, then slowly examining each part of the body she had just revealed.

Damìn watched and was pained, his shame exposed like the box of face powder beside that sinful book: he sensed the fragrance of her powder and could recognize its delicate effusion wafting against the light of the curtain. Within this halo his mother lingered over the last garments.

Vitina came back indoors and caught him spying but said nothing; she just lifted a hand towards him as if to encourage him away from where he was.

NEXT DAY HE MANAGED to get hold of the book, and it didn't take him long to examine it and leaf through it before a note fell from its central pages. He picked it up and found the word Love, and by it a drawing of a heart and a dagger. In his hands was the picture of the Fascist leader's silver dagger, and over that heart it demonstrated all the willingness and capacity to kill.

Damìn put the book back, with the sheet of paper inside, and threw himself onto his sister: he held her tight and kissed her all afternoon, in front of the fig tree, in the fragrant sun-filled garden. The fragrance grew more intense with the heat and ended up infusing itself with the whole enormity that he felt around and within him of his mother's sin. Peering across the wall and looking out towards the river, Damìn understood that deep within him, like the blue sky pushing insistently against the last boundary of the valley, was a pain that was different, continual and ever greater: it was the pain of his mother's beauty.

He began to water the lettuces and the seedlings, and the basil and the pinks, not waiting to do it with his grandfather as he did each evening at dusk. His grandfather returned later than usual and was not surprised to find he had already well watered all the plants. He paused at the fig tree and pressed some of its fruit. He did no more and said nothing, while Damìn waited to be rescued, to be hauled from the depths of the pain that was suffocating him.

AT SUPPER DAMÌN'S MOTHER WAS CALM, more indulgent towards her father-in-law, to whom she turned several times, casually, smiling, each smile different from the other. The grandfather barely replied and moved away from the table as soon as the meal was over, to find more light to read the newspaper. Vitina played with her cutlery and with some crumbs; Grandma carried on eating, cleaning the children's plates with bits of bread.

Damìn's mother relaxed against the back of the chair and undid two buttons on her chest. Damìn could see her breasts as far as the whiter milky circles. He went to get his schoolbook and started to read a poem. But the grammar exercise on the next page made him suddenly remember almost with fear that his father would be back home in two days. Difficult homework and the presence of his father both had the effect of frightening and bewildering him in the face of his own drama and the conjectures and plans he was weaving around it to lessen or cover it up, or simply to keep it away. His father upset everything, he mixed real and unreal, introducing the thorns of another pain, filled with anger and shame.

HE HEARD HIS MOTHER getting out of bed and realized she was sitting at her dressing table. He also seemed to hear the intermittent sound she made when she brushed her hair. He looked at Vitina who was asleep, her hair lying loosely over her pillow in the light from the window. He waited with his eyes open, wide awake, apprehensive. His mother was soon outside her room, and then at the doorway to the garden.

From the half-open window he saw her passing among the flower beds and the trees, and on towards the ruined tower at the end of the garden. He saw her disappear through that very same hole in the wall that was his play-fellow in so many games. He went out into the garden without dressing and climbed onto the fig tree so that he could get over the wall to the riverside and peep into the old building from behind, through the cracks that he knew one by one. His mother was there on the sandy floor, held in Marcacci's embrace.

Marcacci hurriedly undressed her in a perfunctory way. Damìn's pain became all the more acute when he saw his mother had no underwear. The two kissed and then lay down, one on top of the other: his mother beneath, on the sand, with her head and her hair resting on her nightdress; he heard them panting and moaning and tossing about between words and invocations that dissolved into endless sighs.

Damìn was clinging to the wall, struck down by pain and by coldness, shamed before the very wall itself, the bricks that held it up, the cracks through which he was peering; with a shame filled with regret for all the happy and innocent games he had played in that building.

The two lovers meanwhile had changed position and started kissing again. Marcacci had his dagger beside him and a lit cigarette; a wisp of light-blue smoke went straight up towards the roof.

29

Damìn stayed staring at the floor even after his mother had gone, passing once more through the hole. Marcacci dressed carefully, brushing his trousers and jacket and finally fastening his silver dagger self-consciously and with a smile. He left the ruin through the battered door leading to the steps down to the old tannery on the river. Damìn went inside the building to take a closer look at the scene where it had all happened: the ground slightly uneven, smoothed over in several places, like after a game. There was no other trace, no object, no evidence; the ground remained desperately real, firm, familiar; a part of his everyday life that stretched up to the house and down as far as the river and beyond, out into the darkness. He was ashamed of the ground, and of the tears he let fall there.

He returned following the path his mother had taken, as if he might still be able to stop her tracks, or at least wipe them away. He returned not to his own bed but to his sister's, resting against Vitina's warm head while his feelings began to well up from within. Once he had caught his breath, he thought back with great apprehension over what he had seen, frightened of the chasm that now opened before him; and yet little by little a persistent wave of pleasure took hold of his body and mind. Before him, at last, he had the real and immense spectacle of his mother's crime—that which he himself had already imagined and constructed with horror but with stubborn conviction.

NOW THE WHOLE SPECTACLE HELD HIM in its grip, each detail continually unfolding and expanding in the precision of his memory; he had to face up to its truth and its effects. But having to acknowledge and no longer invent it reduced his own sense of guilt, though not his pain.

Soon, though, he would be overwhelmed with anxiety and remorse and no longer able to deal with them alone. For many days, in fact, he associated them with everything around him, with every single flower in the garden, with the clouds and their shapes, with all the sounds that came from the river and from the via Flaminia, along which cars arrived from Rome. He even associated what had happened with the way people moved and talked in the street, with the way they looked at one another and looked at him, or even with the houses along the street; with his grandfather's silence which seemed conscious and sad; even with the behaviour of animals, of the pigeons that came into the garden or the dogs and cats he came across in the street; but above all with the smell of the house that grew with a strange languor, with the taste of food. Every spoonful of the soup his mother had prepared was a portion, an infection of that great scene.

He tried not to look at his mother so as not to detect any too-obvious signs of satisfaction. He even found some clear and consistent sign of that truth, some continuing act of pleasure, in the noise she made in the kitchen, in her words, in her humming, often punctuated with pauses and digressions, which accompanied all she did, and even in the way she opened or closed a door, or gave something to him or his sister, or of lifting or putting down a towel or an undershirt.

He would then go out into the garden and absent-mindedly brush the sand with a finger or with his sandal. He would call Vitina and subject her to cruel games, would push her about and hold her too tightly—he would ruffle her hair, her apron; he would grab her by the knees and push them wide open, would make as if to suffocate her. Vitina didn't run off, didn't complain, nor did she fight back, as if she knew she had to let the brother she adored do these things, so that together they could protect each other from external chaos, from life.

DESPONDENT AND WEIGHED DOWN inside his personal and universal truth, Damìn tried to keep busy helping his grandfather at the clay pit and at the pottery. But here too he found himself interpreting in every action, in every object and shape, the impending and inevitable truth of physical love, its natural fulfilment during each day: its conjunction, its completion, through feeling as well as matter, through juxtaposition and well as intersection, maturation, conquest, conclusion.

Over and above every figure and association—a hoe blade in the clay, the creak of a kiln door, its circular iron lock and bolt, a freshly turned vase, a jug left out to dry, a bowl fresh from the oven, the blaze of the flames seen through the spy hole—the greatest and most unjustified love was still that of his mother and Marcacci the Fascist leader, the handsome conqueror, a man of dauntless courage, even a killer. Behind the amorous evidence of every image, he expected to see Marcacci's face, his whole figure, his dagger immediately before him. From the mouth of every vase came the unctuous *ahs*, the blood-filled *uhs* and *ohs* of his mother's sighs.

His grandfather saw the boy had little enthusiasm for work and told him he should go home and read instead. The suggestion was not meant unkindly since the old man was still heartened by the signs his grandson had shown of being a born potter, a true Damiano, an artist, following the way in which the Possanza family alternated in vocations and roles from generation to generation.

DAMÌN FELT AN URGE to widen his group of friends and the world around him, which had now been reduced to that scene inside the garden ruin. He tried to become more friendly with his classmates; he started going to the playgrounds in other parts of town; he even went a couple of times to the parish club.

One Saturday afternoon, just before the end of the second term, he went running at the sports ground where many boys of his own age would meet, together with grown-ups. There he saw Marcacci, bare-chested, wearing khaki shorts, and on his head a Fascist fez. He was enjoying the sun and giving out orders here and there to everyone, athletes as well as spectators. The ubiquitous dagger shone at his waist, and his black flaming gaze made him look squint-eyed, as though he were driven by a higher force, of beauty, of power and the brutality of authority.

Damìn remained there transfixed, mesmerized by his gestures. He was dragged out of it by a boy from his street, just as if he had been pulled out of a trance. Damìn was thankful and said as much, to the extent that the boy wanted him to pay for the cinema and an extra present of two Popolari cigarettes and a Moresca liquorice drop in return. Damìn hurriedly paid out the two lire his grandfather had given him, regarding the money as epitomizing his family and all of his unbearable sorrow. The cinema made him feel better and he stayed to watch the second show, beyond supper time.

ON OTHER DAYS HE ENDED UP sitting with friends from the lower end of town on the stone steps down to the

workshop of Amilcare Occhialini, the cobbler, who sat
there behind his table, shaggy-haired and half-naked. A
large leather apron covered his chest and most of his
body: sticking out from it were his black hands that
pulled the thread and manoeuvred the skiving knife
around the soles and the uppers with such certainness
and precision that from them he could immediately
produce objects recognizable as shoes.

It was a labour that Damìn could watch, making
no associations with the image, the film, of his own
truth, since the shoemaker was expert and determined,
and talked away as he worked: he told stories about his
life in France, commented on life there in the town of
Fossombrone, talked about politics and work and often,
at regular intervals, he mocked and scorned the Fascists,
even the Duce, Rome, the King and the Fatherland.
And when it came to God and the clergy he laughed
out loud, shaking his head and driving in an extra rivet.

Damìn now went every day to the steps of the
workshop and sometimes went down to sit on a low
straw stool beside Occhialini, like an assistant. He
remained there listening, each time persuaded, touched
by a truth, however small, different and distant from his
own truth.

Occhialini admired his grandfather, who likewise
much respected him as a master shoemaker and as a communist and antifascist, more anarchist than communist in

truth. Occhialini was so open-minded and had such wide experience because he had gone off when he was still only fourteen to work in France, to Lyon, and then into Switzerland, to Geneva. He had come back to bury his mother, his only relative in the world, being the son of a 'father unknown', and he had been forced to remain in Italy by new government regulations on emigration. He had always been against Fascism, and when Giacomo Matteotti was assassinated in 1924 he'd had the courage to speak out in the town square against the Duce and against the monarchy. He always had a few books on the table beside him and would recite the latest poem he had learnt or the latest piece of history to all the boys who came to visit. He always followed with some appropriate comment that was instructive and edifying.

'Puppet of the capitalist bourgeoisie' was how he had once described Mussolini to Damìn's grandfather when he had stopped by at the workshop to see him and had been surprised to see his grandson among the children there.

'Quite right,' his grandfather had said. 'Puppet he is, and the puppet master certainly isn't the King.'

'At most, the King is the manager,' Occhialini had added, 'the one who does the organizing and hires out the premises. The puppet master is capital.'

'Careful! Don't start getting these boys into trouble.'

'No, no, just the right dose ... and anyway, they see real work here, and that's always a good thing. It's school that ruins them. The radio, political rallies, parish youth club.'

Occhialini was an ugly man and yet he was often talking about women, especially his love affairs with French women. According to him, they particularly liked making love with Italians, without too much coaxing and flattery, and with much glee.

Occhialini coloured and spiced his stories with a certain liberty, though never vague or superficial since he was conscious of teaching the boys, and teaching about things of prime importance. All the boys were of an age when they would begin to recognize desire and start to think of little else in anticipation of their first encounter, of the fateful, miraculous occasion of the first experience. Damìn was the youngest of them and said nothing. But he found the cobbler's chats helpful, and from them he obtained particular words and details that helped him to order and arrange his own great truth.

Once he went as far as asking: 'But is it right that women have to enjoy it as well?'

'Of course,' exclaimed Occhialini, 'women as well! They too are alive and free, and if you want daughters of the Lord ... of the earth, of love, they too have a body and ... even their own special organ for making love. Between their legs they have their sweet, warm, beautiful cunt, hairy and open, which is never to be denied or hidden and even worse ignored, but is to be looked at, touched, parted lip from lip between the fingers or with the cock, and if you are already a man, grown up and well experienced, even with the nose and with the tongue—especially if there's real love, real feeling and cleanliness. This would send French women into ecstasy, for we Italians are not afraid of looking at their cunt and even kissing and licking it. Otherwise what is it, other than a bit of leather, a hole, or like a shoe that you slip on? . . . Even a shoe has to be admired! Women have to get enjoyment like men, and more so, out of social justice and as a reward for giving birth . . . The skill of a man isn't so much in how big and hard it is and the number of times he's able to fuck . . . but in the act of helping and serving a woman, in making her enjoy it, in having the honesty to enjoy her fine body . . . all, all of her body.

'I know . . . I know that the bourgeoisie conquer, exploit and then cast aside. But they are landlords and petty businessmen blinded by prejudice, by false pride and by the Church . . . they are the Fascist pimps who make love only with the whores who submit to them, or in brothels, the true churches for their immature twisted souls, for their animal pride . . . bullied, cuckolded by true cuckolds. So, boys, you must learn to be free, and make sure you always lead the young girl on with kindness, that you always love her, that you make her share your pleasure and that afterwards you respect her more than before . . . and if she has given it to you, thank her with affection.

'Poor women, what courage they have to find to give themselves to a man, even just once! All hell and earth is unleashed against them. How many of them, nearly all, have to submit to their husband who comes home and mounts them like a cockerel and cares nothing for them—he even pretends it's nothing. He has his way with her . . . he alone . . . treating her like a dog! And remember that women are almost always better than men, cleverer and more generous—almost always. In France, in Switzerland and even in Germany, always, that's for sure: the women are better than the men, also more just and more intelligent—better workers too. They screw more freely than they do here. Whenever they wish and whenever it gives them pleasure—with bodily and mental passion, with no fear, or regret, or false modesty. They give great satisfaction to any man who knows how to take them . . . and then he really feels powerful and at peace, capable of doing great things, and not just in bed. The world will be fairer and more beautiful when all of today's jerking off and fingering becomes contented fucking.'

III

The Master's Workshop. Luana, the Virgin Queen.
When Is a Woman a Whore?

NOT A DAY WOULD PASS without Damìn turning up at
Occhialini's workshop soon after lunch, to spend the
early hours of the afternoon alone with him. The others arrived later, after they had been for a run around
the field and watched the girls doing gymnastics in
their shorts, or been for a dive in the river beyond the
Roman bridge, where the washerwomen went and
swayed their bottoms as they pounded their washing
on the rocks with their dresses hitched halfway up their
thighs: and beside them their daughters, or girls from
out of town, who washed their legs, their necks and
their arms in their underclothes among the white rocks
before the waterfall; and then stayed there in the sun,
some with no bras or even underpants.

The boys would squat down among the reeds and
watch and masturbate, all in a circle, and then re-
emerge shouting and joking in the splendour of the
afternoon. One of them had found a pair of light-blue
women's knickers, laid out over a bush, left there in
who–knows–what sinful hurry, with flowery lace all

around them, the cloth reinforced along the central strip, front and back—worn and even a little frayed. All of them had jerked off for a second time, in the same circle, frantically competing for that garment, and had then hidden it away for future gatherings.

'TALK TO THE GIRLS, approach them,' said Occhialini. 'Smile at them, say hello—whether they're from out of town or not, whether they're from school or not. You can be sure they're just as bored, always in the same group. They'd enjoy the company of a few bright, clever boys. Invite them for an outing above the Capuchin friary or the fields towards Sant'Ippolito . . . go and gather some corncobs and roast them by the riverbank.'

Damìn felt more nervous when the other boys were there. He'd greet them all but would then start eyeing them one by one, noting how fortunate and contented they were; then he would go back to watching them again as a group and envying them all for being fortunate with their mothers, and happy and equal as a group, able to jerk off all together with no feeling of shame or fear; able to chase after the girls; to talk to them, joke with them, even insult them, pushing them into doorways and hugging them tightly in secret corners of the town's alleyways, and even in the streets. For him it would have been impossible to go down even the emptiest and darkest alleyway: if he tried to think of anything of that kind it went against the very reality of existence—the alleyway, made by man and a part of human life . . . a reality that took him back to his own reality, dominated by the great drama that would never allow him to forget his own part, would never allow him to put on stage any other woman who was not his mother, or any other sexual encounter that did not turn straightaway into that between his mother and Marcacci. The darkness of the blindest alleyway would be dispelled by the light streaming in through the chinks of the ruin, those fixed dazzling lights that drew him to that great stage; and likewise no splendour could be any other than that reflected on his mother's mirror at whatever hour of the day or night. Her fate rebounded on him and kindled the pain within his breast: total pain, unhappiness. If he tried to understand it, in his desperate attempt to get away from its constant grasp, like a lizard from a circle of fire, his unhappiness became the implacable and ever-present truth in his being, in the being of Damiano Possanza, grandson of Damiano Possanza the master potter, Damiano son of Dorino and the flesh and blood of Norma Coramboni, the blonde from out of town, the beautiful woman from Urbino.

He had to get away, to run off into the main square to buy his comic, *L'Avventuroso*, and then to wait for evening, alone, at the first bend of the via Flaminia, watching the cars go by. Not all of them came from

Rome and not all of them were black; a few that drove
past were red open-topped sports cars with some
young fair-haired driver wearing a blue or checked
jersey. There was always someone looking for marks left
by the great wheels of the Duce's car, the Alfa Romeo
that had roared past a few days earlier—going so fast
that those fortunate bystanders along the road could
hardly catch a glimpse of Mussolini's great eyes with
their constant piercing gaze, flashing like a sword. Then
from behind they had seen his elbow jutting from his
cape as he turned the sharp bend and vanished in a
flash, like a miracle.

But Damìn's full sense of pain was brought back to
him by the river below, with its constantly flowing
waters and rock pools that watched and remembered
everything, and the current further down in which,
towards the banks, were glassy pools of water with their
all-seeing mirrors and telltale reflections below the
garden and below the ruined tower.

L'Avventuroso gave him some consolation and
distracted him with its voyages through space. These
far-off and mysterious journeys inspired him and he
felt his strong pristine body drawn to the eternal youth
of Luana, the virgin queen.

NONE OF THE TREES along the riverbanks could be
compared with those of Luana's kingdom. Only a few

meagre clumps of long reeds or canes could resemble the savannah that stretched beyond the jungle, far away from the tracks of the native bearers.

Damìn followed his group of companions, not all of whom he knew, who went ahead in ones and twos, but in well-established formation.

They climbed the right bank further down the river, through the canes and into the fields so that they could arrive unseen at the edge of the rock pools before the bridge where the girls went to bathe. They began shouting as soon as they heard and caught sight of the girls, and crouched among the bushes. Soon they began masturbating, shouting and swearing. Damìn stayed some distance away and could barely watch, pent up with disgust, his hands clenched and hidden behind his back, almost afraid of being infected by the gestures and the proximity of the other boys. His companions were jeering and chanting at the girls, waggling their dicks. The girls kicked about in the water expecting the boys to come down into the river. When they saw no sign of them they moved further on, but then came straight back to the bank, to the place where they could hear the boys squawking, and came in a little closer. The boys, hearing them approaching, gesticulated and swore all the more.

'What are you doing?' asked the girls, who had stopped at the last point from which they still couldn't see.

'Ah, ah,' yelled the boys. 'We've found a dickybird, nesting here. And we're looking after it, and making it good and hard, with our hands until it's nice and stiff, until it starts drooling and dribbling.'

'What dickybird? Is it small, can it fly . . . it is big? Has it fallen from its nest or is it injured? Is it a water bird? Can we come and see it?' asked some of the girls, amid the shrieks of the others.

'Yes,' replied the proudest of the boys, without a second thought; but he himself was taken aback when he saw the group of girls appear among the canes.

'Look,' said the oldest boy, getting up from where he had been lying on the sand and displaying his erect cock, while he pulled up two other boys whose trousers were also unbuttoned, with their dicks out.

'Ugh, disgusting! What are you doing? You filthy lot! Perverts!' shouted some of the girls, though they neither moved away nor lowered their gaze.

'You're sick,' said another girl, moving back into the canes.

'Ah, ah,' cried the boys in proud defiance. They were masturbating even faster, straining forward with their tongues between their teeth. The girls carried on watching, with occasional exclamations of disgust that might have seemed like admiration, or even pleasure.

DAMÌN WATCHED HORRIFIED from his position further away, fearing all the girls would suddenly faint at this outrageous sight.

But instead they remained—recalcitrant, hesitant, but present. And none of the girls were as far away as he: none, not even the youngest, those with pigtails and light-blue petticoats.

The ground between the boys and the girls remained firm: on the one side, the frantic gesticulation and cries among the dry canes; on the other, the coloured undulation of the reflections in the water behind.

Damìn's natural urge to escape was far greater than any feeling towards his companions. But he was taken aback by the cries of the boys shouting out to watch more carefully and come closer. 'The dicky-bird's eaten. The dickybird's drooling, drooling! Look what a dribble . . . what a string of pearls.'

'What is it?' some of the girls asked, those furthest away. Some were crouching, as if to hide themselves.

'Ah, ah. Here it is, here it is,' the boys repeated. 'Come and see the pearls, come and take the necklaces . . . then you'll find out.'

The girls ran off confused. One of them, a brunette, took two paces towards the boys and lifted her petticoat to let them see her knickers.

'If I showed you this, you'd die straight away,' she said, and flounced off.

The boys were shocked indeed by the sight, and all they could do was utter a few frantic lonely sighs.

The girls all went back in a group towards the river, running their hands through their hair, thrusting their knees back into the water.

Damìn quickly vanished among the vegetation higher up along the bank. He noticed how, after the canes, there were willows and how the brambles were creeping into the sand. In some of the almost-waterless pools along the river edge he could see the sky and the clouds floating across high above. Meanwhile he tried to give himself some wise, serious counsel, acknowledging that those riverbanks had the misfortune to be barren. It seemed he could draw one principle from their wild confusion: desperation will take over the whole world, by force of being desperate, and then there will no longer be difference, nor pain.

He stopped halfway along the bank and seemed to feel the movement of the earth beneath his feet.

SUPPER WAS EATEN IN SILENCE when Damìn's father was at home, especially if he had come back earlier than usual. He generally returned later in the evening, as if on purpose, after the dishes had been washed and while Damìn and Vitina were getting ready for bed.

Granddad and Grandma were already in their room. He would eat his meal cold at one corner of the dining table, now covered once more with its velvet cloth designed with a picture of a green oasis under a blue starry sky: in exact coloured chequers, yet solid in its detail, like the map of a small realm.

For years this cloth had been the field on which Damìn could play out his fears and his fantasies, its spaces changing according to his mood. His father sat eating and pondering, occupying the fortress tower in a part of the desert on the other side of the oasis. That fortress now belonged to him: the very same colour, dotted with peepholes and words unspoken, with a central tower that resembled the ruin at the bottom of the garden.

Standing behind him, Damìn raised his hand in contempt at the back of his father's head, with an urge to strike it, to fracture it, to kill the man. To control the impulse he took hold of Vitina, and watched her fall asleep in his arms, finding it difficult to hold her, still in the grip of parricidal desire. Then he lay in bed waiting, gazing up at the ceiling. Through the shutters he imagined what was happening outside in the garden and in the river and up on the road towards the town. In the same way, he would see on the bedroom ceiling the movements of his mother as she crossed the garden towards the ruin. Once the movements had stopped, leaving a solid darkness, as alive as a teeming swarm of bees, he would get out of bed and go down to his observation post.

One evening he saw his mother kneeling, naked to the waist, her face buried beneath Marcacci's belt. He was standing, arms thrust forward, looking every bit a soldier. Suddenly he took hold of her by the hair and pulled her further in, against his stomach.

Damìn could see only his mother's bare rounded shoulders under her loose mop of hair, between the hands of his mighty enemy. Marcacci groaned, moving and clasping the full mass of hair in front of him. All of a sudden the woman looked up, her face catching the moonlight, wet from forehead to chin. She stayed in that position beneath the ever-whiter light; meanwhile the enemy buttoned up his trousers and readjusted his dagger—its mother-of-pearl handle glinting in front, against Damìn's mother's mouth.

Marcacci turned and left in a hurry with hardly a goodbye, pressing a finger against his nose as a recommendation of silence. Damìn's mother remained there on her knees, not moving, still looking up and without drying herself. Damìn waited too. After much time, during which the light had already changed twice, as if to scrutinize more pitilessly her face, her whole head and the dishevelled mass of hair that fell down to her waist, she stood up again. But before going back through the hole in the wall, she wandered around inside as if searching desperately for some other way out.

ONCE BACK IN HIS ROOM, Damìn threw himself on Vitina's bed; he watched her breathing calmly and gently in her sleep. But he was soon driven into his own bed by the urge to masturbate, his face in his pillow, his hands and his penis frantic, his eyes tightly closed and tearful.

Early next morning he appeared at the doorway of Occhialini's workshop, which was still only half-open. The cobbler was holding a parcel of fish he had just bought and was looking to see how fresh it was. The fish shone wet and white, pearly . . . Damìn looked at it, as if . . . and tried to avoid the horrible comparison, which was such that he couldn't speak and ran off without even saying hello.

He went into the main square and hung around for at least two hours by the newsstands, and then here and there along the porticoes. He watched the pigeons and chose one of them that might be carrying a message for him. But when it looked as if the pigeon really was about to swoop down towards him, he got out of the way and ran into the flock so that they all scattered in fright and his messenger was lost among them.

TOWARDS MIDDAY HE WENT BACK to Occhialini and found him alone, working away with awl and thread.

'Did you hear the Duce's speech?' he began.

'What's he been saying this time?' asked Occhialini. 'More playacting to stun the world?'

'Is it true they even listen to him abroad?'

'Of course. But with contempt, not respect . . . perhaps even with fear, alarm . . . '

'But are they really better than us abroad, like you say?'

'Yes. Pretty well everywhere.'

'And the women?'

'As well.'

'They make love more freely?'

'Yes.'

'Every time they want to?'

'Yes.'

The shortness of the answer brought Damìn straight to the question he wanted to ask.

'And those who are married?'

'Just the same.'

'A married woman can also make love with someone else?' He tried to be as clear as he could, despite his inner reticence to talk about that particular matter.

'Yes, of course.'

51

'But isn't it seen as wrong, even abroad?'

'Yes, but not like here. The woman is freer.'

'And they make love in all kinds of ways?'

'Yes, of course.'

'And they're not seen as whores?'

'Yes and no. It depends.'

'Depends on what?'

'On the husband, for example, or on who the other man is, or the family circumstances . . . if she's short of money or forced to do it.'

'But a woman like that, she's always a whore!'

'Maybe. Though not necessarily. Perhaps she doesn't love her husband . . . or perhaps he doesn't satisfy her, or even ignores her or treats her badly.'

'But if a married woman goes with a handsome powerful young man and only to . . . to . . . screw . . . then she really is a whore!'

'She might also be unhappy, naive, weak-minded or just ambitious.'

'But if the man is powerful . . . if he's a Fascist?'

'Then she might just be the victim . . . trapped, ignorant.' Occhialini had caught his train of thought, and continued on in a less forthright tone. 'She has to be warned, she must be made to understand that this man is nothing . . . she has to be told, persuaded that he's taking mean advantage of her . . . that when he loses interest . . . soon . . . soon . . . because these types are never really great lovers . . . they're just loudmouths, exhibitionists. When he doesn't want her any more, he'll even put her to shame.'

'But how can she be warned?'

'Ah, that's not at all easy. Perhaps it's not even possible. It's important to keep with her, look after her. To support her, to help her at work, in her life, in everything . . . even in understanding herself better.'

'Of course. Her children, for example, they could do something.' Damìn tried to show he was capable of thinking objectively about such things, even about an idea so extreme, so close to what was really happening in Fossombrone. 'But I think they'd want to disown a mother like that . . . or at least forget her, if not kill her.'

'No, no, goodness gracious. That's the very worst that can happen. Blind suffering, proud revenge . . . . such things destroy everything—and most of all the weakest and the most innocent, the children.

'Children have to try to love their mother even more,' continued Occhialini. 'They have to understand her, talk to her, make her see they are good and they care about her. They have to remember their mother is not the Virgin Mary . . . that there isn't and never was a Virgin Mary, at least not among mothers. They have to remember she's a woman, with the body of a woman and with an honest desire for a man . . . and that she has conceived and borne these children through love, through making love.

'Betrayal . . . pride, revenge! Goodness gracious, they're ideas and feelings belonging to a past age, to ignorant people, a backward society.

'Fascism and the Church still cultivate these prejudices to keep people under their thumb, in fear—never free, never . . . no one . . . no one is free even with their own cocks and cunts, or even with their own labour or their own ideals.'

His way of talking was ponderous and insistent, his self-taught rhetoric naive and revolutionary, full of examples and references, and much like the prying gossiping tone of those from the lower parts of Fossombrone where he lived.

IV

*School.*Vermutte *and Vermouth. What a Prick*

DURING EACH NEW ENCOUNTER in the ruined tower, Damìn saw his mother involving herself with greater and more frenzied passion. Often she spoke fast and long and her words ended in floods of tears. She would then complain at length between sobs. Marcacci stood watching her, impatient, rapping his hand beside his dagger.

His mother's humiliation was greater each time. Damìn even enjoyed the suffering he saw so clearly expressed, though he couldn't understand its reason; he enjoyed it because he felt its deep unhappiness. But why should his mother despair when Marcacci still turned up just the same, always dressed the same and always with his dagger, and when he still undressed her each time and kissed her and pushed her down beneath him?

This doubt took away some of Damìn's pain, giving him the pleasure of imagining that his mother was suffering through her awareness that she was betraying him, Damìn, as well as his whole family, his home, the world.

Occhialini's words and understanding were no longer enough, not least because school had restarted and Damìn saw him less frequently. In the classroom he stared for hours at the large window that looked across to the wall of San Rocco, or instead at the blank, empty blackboard. The rectangular spaces of both were of a size that could be multiplied to contain the pain as well as the vertiginous fixity of his gaze. Its fixity, then its fall. A fixity that then dropped, as if from flight, falling for hours without ever touching anything; and slowing down, gliding; falling, then regaining height with successive gusts of air, without ever crashing or touching the ground. It was endless . . . and yet what was endless at school was the hostility.

The schoolmistress couldn't stand him and had placed him at the back, at a desk pushed precariously against the second door of the schoolroom to keep it shut. Across this door was an iron bar, secured by a padlock. Damìn spent hours fingering the lock and its shackle.

Of all that he was taught, he could just about follow Fucini's stories about the Tuscan countryside.

ONE DAY THE TEACHER MADE the brighter pupils take it in turns to read aloud, and asked him to continue reading from the point where one of the girls, the daughter of Onorati the lawyer, had broken down

breathless with excitement. Damìn started off well, at
the right point, though his voice trembled. He read the
story of Vermutte the cart driver. The word *Vermutte*
was written in italics each time he came across it, unlike
all the other words on the page; obviously to emphasize
something. That was how he interpreted it, and so he
read the word *Vermutte* emphasizing the sound of the
final double *t*. The teacher soon stopped him:

'Oh, oh, that's quite wrong . . . how do we read it?
Possanza, alas, is not familiar with French. Foreign lan-
guages are not his strong point. How do we read this
word? How is it correctly pronounced?'

'*Vermuth*,' the lawyer's daughter immediately
answered, back once again in full form.

'That's right, *vermuth*,' repeated the teacher. And
shaking her head and stroking the hairs on her narrow
lips, she added: 'I don't suppose our Possanza has any
vermuth in his house, eh! He won't be familiar with this
liquor.'

Damìn was shocked by the injustice, and her final
comment returned him to deep suffering, for he felt
exposed before everyone in his unworthiness and
shame, together with his whole family and his house.
And it made no difference that the accusation was
unjust; on the contrary, its injustice made his pain and
guilt even greater. What the teacher and all the class was
doing was certainly wrong, but the wrong was directed

deliberately at him, and with impunity, because everyone knew he would have to submit to it. And the implications in terms of dialect over the pronunciation of a particular word concerned a whole town, an entire region and beyond, in the middle of which stood Fossombrone, with its river and its houses.

Wounded, he turned to the door and to the padlock, and after a few moments rested his head on the desk. He began to masturbate through the broken pocket of his trousers. He banged his hard dick against the desk and, as he stroked it, recited the following little scene:

' "Who is knocking?" A bit too loud though, and then in jest, in a rather unseemly manner . . . "Who is it" ', all in the same quiet voice.

' "What a prick!" ' he suddenly replied out loud. ' "What a prick!" '

' "This prick. The ruler, the king." ' In just the way he would have liked to behave or to command: the blind griefless ruler, the true and obstinate superior, the master of liberty, leader of the anti-school, espouser of good wise industrious ignorance, keeper of the clock that keeps no track of time, keeper of the real time of the countryside and of the river.

' "What a prick!" ' sighed Damìn; but already he was losing interest and he turned to another occupation, drawn by eternal guilt.

HIS RESENTMENT TOWARDS the schoolmistress and towards all his friends, the whole class, was physical: he felt it towards everyone on the other side of the via Flaminia, the town's rich powerful families, it's smart society, those who strolled about the main square, who sat in its cafes, went in and out of the town's social club, went to the theatre, drove about in a motor car, drank tea as well as vermouth.

The girls in his class were only interested in boys from the Duce's middle classes, the favourites, the brightest, the successful ones, and exchanged messages with them, and gifts and encouraging glances.

In the other corner at the back of the class, in continual agitation, was the only boy with whom Damìn had any fellow feeling; he had had to retake the year and came from a remote country part, travelling by train. He already had the beginnings of a beard and spent all his time drawing penises on every sheet of paper, on the cover of every book, on every blank space. Erect penises, foreskin pulled back, with open wings halfway up the shaft and a musket around its neck with fixed bayonet. He even had the nerve to draw them on pieces of paper and send them to the girls, waiting for their reaction with a ready grin, with insinuations and other more evident signs of encouragement.

One morning, in the broad freedom of the religious-education hour, he added three of his pubic hairs to a card. He generally preferred to send these messages to the most beautiful girl, the prison governor's daughter, a southerner with shiny reddish-black hair. She made no reply but Damìn caught her several times looking back at him—Jenner—as he was looking down and drawing his ubiquitous design. He had even begun to carve it on his desk—at first underneath, but then also on the flap and on either side of the inkwell.

Cerignola finally replied with a card smeared red, either with rouge make-up or a mauve pencil: a small card with a single red smudge in the middle, no words or other marks. But for Jenner it must have meant a great deal because that morning he sent messages of every kind to Cerignola, even gifts of fruit and flowers he had picked on his way to school, and a small ring; and then one day a piece of blotting paper with all the drops of his masturbation, once again during the hour of religion.

Damìn admired Jenner and felt inferior, lacking his shamelessness and his marvellous ability to act fearlessly, with no sense of guilt. He could just about compensate for this in essays that were supposed to be fiction, into which he threw himself wholeheartedly, using all he knew and could invent and imagine. But the teacher told him the essays had been copied, that they were not his own work, that his ordinary brain, the brain of a potter's boy from the river, couldn't hold expressions and ideas like the ones he was writing down. Damìn became increasingly humiliated and had to withdraw into the darkest spaces of his sorrow.

AT THE END OF THE SECOND TERM, the teacher dictated a choice of two subjects for a composition to be written in class: the first on friendship, relating to a story they had just read about Euryalus and Nisus, and the second on Italy's great destiny under the new leadership of Rome.

Damìn started right away, eager to write both, inspired by many ideas on each of them.

In the first composition he imagined that Jenner, one misty morning on his way to school, had been hit by a train and had lost both legs. He described the accident on two sides of paper and spent another page writing about his friend's despair, his pain and the hopeless depression that tormented him, right up to his determination to give up and die.

Each page was full of poetic thoughts on nature and pervaded by a cosmic vapour that settled around the figure of his friend's mother. The detailed description of this woman and her purity was established through the whirl of time, the unfortunate accident and the feelings it produced. This part was an introduction before the appearance of the power of friendship, his friendship. Damìn maintained contact between his injured friend and the school, kept him company, comforted him, arranged for him to meet up with the girl he loved: he even designed him a pair of automatic legs from his knowledge of the space machines in *L'Avventuroso* comics and visits to the workshop of a mechanic on the via Flaminia. Above all, he helped and comforted his friend's mother with a feeling of complete trust, something he could never experience in his relationship with his own mother.

In the end, with rejoicing for a liberation more his own than that of the friend he had restored to health, they return to school, to the classroom, arm in arm, to the admiration of all.

At the party that followed, he and Jenner offered cakes and drinks and several bottles of vermouth with labels on which was clearly written: 'Vermouth. Sweet wine commonly known as *Vermutte.*' He even went as far as writing that during the party he noticed, when he was finally able to see one of his classmates (a lawyer's daughter whose name, however, he didn't reveal) from close and with no distinction of class, she had blue eyes and blushed as she shook his hand.

In the second essay he found the opportunity to throw in Occhialini's truths, but turning their meaning upside down. He described how this man belonged to a bygone age of communists who had no fatherland and no religion, who had no ideals apart from resentment and hatred of material pleasure in life.

He could also mix together Marcacci and the Duce: on the one hand, Damìn could distance that mighty figure from himself and his home, entrusting him to the leadership of Rome; and on the other, he could raise him to a level that seemed unreal, or at least high above that reality that involved Marcacci, Damìn's mother and everything around them.

On those sheets of school paper, at his desk, in a classroom atmosphere that was detached, almost abstract, he could draw upon that unutterable feeling of admiration, emulation and even a desire to be equal, to understand his enemy, an urge that ran loose within him like an illness and that seethed from time to time inside his head, his arms, his breath; a feeling he had never even wanted to admit, let alone express: not even in the battles and among the ranks of the goodies and baddies in *L'Avventuroso*.

From there, the physical attraction he felt for the handsome centurion, for his body, his bearing, his whole manner: his gaze, his confidence, his general command over himself and others; that dagger that might have looked better fastened to the Duce's belt, with its whole hilt on display, in mother-of-pearl, topped by the clear sharp gilt profile of the eagle.

He could pour out all his feelings of submission as well as the desire to be wounded by that eagle's beak, and then the hope in the end of being able to grasp hold of it, to find contentment and fulfilment in the perfection of the other. Marcacci the Duce held Italy by its hair, urging it, guiding it, nurturing it. The Duce became tall and handsome, with a mass of black curls that bristled with his brilliant thoughts. He was a powerful athlete, victorious at sport and in the public square, in the stadium and in his political and strategic discourse. Under him the nation became finer than any other in the world, especially France and Switzerland, where the immorality of free pleasure sapped every force of integrity, whether civil or military. The Duce would soon be visiting Fossombrone, passing through the Furlo tunnel, excavated with the skill and might of Roman chisels, and would be stopping at the sports ground. There he would embrace all the winners of the games held in his honour. His embrace had the tone of a lyrical composition, in all its intrinsic truth and emotion, even as far as the intimacy of both bodies: those of the leader and the victorious devoted adolescent.

Half of the last page contained a celebration of the beauty of the river Metauro that crossed the city and the plains, down to the sea which was once again *mare nostrum*, a part of Imperial Rome. And the emperor was *Traiano*, Trajan.

DAMÌN MANAGED TO COMPLETE both compositions, leaving them by the small gold clock the teacher had placed on the desk to show the amount of time left. She picked them up and examined them with surprise, but not without commenting, with her usual sarcastic smile, the smile that inevitably appeared on her wrinkled face on those mercifully few occasions when she had to speak to Possanza, that the only pupils to tackle both subjects would be those incapable of writing one alone, those who couldn't decide, those whose ideas were so confused that they were just as valid for one as for the other and therefore devoid of any true meaning. Damìn was so pleased with his compositions that he still remained hopeful, almost confident.

But the new wave of disappointment was greater than his twenty-four hours of hope, and it soon crashed upon him in front of the whole class, as total and inevitable as the constant light that shone from the lamp on the teacher's desk, as all the air in the classroom plus that which bore in on the windows from outside.

'The compositions of a hothead, a boy ravaged by dreams that are impossible, turbid, or at least too big for him.

'Many words,' she continued, 'indeed many phrases, whole phrases, must have been copied from some illicit book he has happened across, not a schoolbook, yet used with no discernment or measure. And what did he mean about "no distinctions of class"? On the train such distinctions certainly exist! Even at school. Yes, my boy. You need to be intelligent and work hard to move up from the second to the third year. And don't imagine that the Duce, concerned about leading the destiny of the world, would ever have the time, let alone the inclination, to embrace a young boy from Fossombrone who wins on the sports field. And there again what competition could you possibly ever win to be embraced even by a local dignitary, let alone the Duce?'

That lesson too would nevertheless be learnt in the end, in that same obscure way that reality and the world of others would always, at the appropriate moment, conspire against him, against the whole weight of his sorrows, plans, desires, needs, thoughts, actions, expectations, hopes, dreams . . . even against the sandals he wore, the handkerchief in his pocket, his bread, his money.

V

A Convict's Picture. Manaccia.
The Javelin. The Suspicion

JUST OUTSIDE THE CITY was a stretch of the river down-
stream that seemed to Damìn to be struck by some disease: the water groaned more loudly in many black
whirls and frothed against a high stone wall that stood
alone, curved, with no road above it, nor houses. On
the open land there must have been an abandoned vegetable plot, at the far end of which likely lay the foot
of the prison walls.

One afternoon Damìn had wandered down that far
with the usual company and, encouraged by the pristine
sun of a fine mid-September day, he scaled the first part
of the turret, stone by stone, and then skirted around
the top, balancing over a broken low wall that rose in
random levels of brick, between luxuriant and hardy
vegetation, which at a certain point rose until it reached
the final parapet with the last few steps and plants. Above
it was an actual abandoned vegetable plot, with its paths
still visible between the weeds and debris; and at the
far end, as he had expected, stood the outer wall of
the prison. Prominent at the centre of the steel-grey

rendering was the bright blue form of a plastered arch-way, a little larger than a door, and just as deep as a porch.

Damìn approached, and inside he saw the drawn figures of a naked man and woman at eye level, one in front of the other: the man with a large hard cock, she with rounded tits and dark nipples. Her navel, below, was marked in the same manner as her nipples. Further down still, her cunt, broad and hairy, drawn in black and red, seeming open, split—all split, indeed throbbing and frothy.

Damìn paused for some time in front of the figure, considering it as a whole and in every part—every detail of the drawing as well as the material used for drawing it. He read even a smirk of pleasure and defi-ance in the faces of the two, though merely hinted at by a thick outline: that of the woman accompanied by two streaks of charcoal that represented her hair.

It made the woman's face seem broader and clearer, and in its broadness her sense of guilt increased. Between the lines of charcoal the plaster changed colour with many shades and marks that gave the actual appearance of folds of skin. The man's cock was filled out, insistently, in black—erect and unnaturally big, disproportionate to the same sinful intent. It was closed by an enormous foreskin, less black, coloured by a single charcoal line; parting from its tip, a slim strip of blueness and lime went straight up towards the top. The strip continued up, dwindling rapidly until it was lost high up, interrupted by small patches of colour and lime. It seemed to Damìn almost as though it penetrated the cement of the archway and then the prison wall.

Those figures must have been drawn by a convict, a murderous womanizer. The woman's cunt, drawn front-on by the convict, was now at the same height as the boy's face: broad, real, with the vivid red at the centre of the dribbling slit. It was not the red of charcoal, nor of pencil, nor of paint: it looked just like blood at the enquiry that Damìn turned around anxiously in his mind. He thought for a moment that it might have dribbled from some flower or fruit the murderer had crushed in his fingers; but, now in the grip of fear, he held to the plain evidence of blood. What blood? That of the murderer, or of the woman he was making love to, first violated and possessed, then killed? Moving closer to the figures with his fingers touching the plaster here and there, he even thought of the menstrual fluid of an innocent girl, taken prisoner, or of a nun. He sniffed the rounded organ and its centre but drew back in disgust, gripped by a sudden revulsion. The red must be a mixture of blood and menstrual fluid: of mysterious muslin, jam rags and cloths, gauzes and bandages down to the ankles.

HE CONTINUED TO STUDY each agglomeration and transparency of colour. Each marginal trace, close beneath where the drops of red had dripped and fallen following the natural line of descent, beyond the picture and as far as the ground: indeed beyond the time of those figures, up to that moment when he found himself there in front of it; and beyond, for ever.

This continuity that overwhelmed him made his scrutiny even more detailed, directing him towards his most intimate motivations, as far as exploring the sense of his own ignorance, even his extraneousness. The black-and-red organ, oval and dense, emerged from the composition and struck him as the most exact revelation he had hitherto been given about female genitals. He wanted to laugh at the turgid male and his presumptuous streak, noting his stick legs, the half-consumed buttock, like that of a dead unburied corpse found after months on the riverbank: a wicked little man swept away by the current of the river Metauro.

He avoided the brazen face of the woman that looked like the foul face of a brothel whore. He went beyond the tits and the navel, pools and bends of the eddy of a secondary current, destined to be lost among the canes and the sand of a broader bank leaving round traces over the background and stones of uncertain colour.

From the red-and-black circle of his inspection on that bright afternoon, whose sun was all the more intense for being out of season, he was distracted only by the blue roundness of the sky over Fossombrone.

When the light began to make him squint, his gaze fell on the towers of the prison, on the city walls. He was moved by the power of all the town's buildings, the number of roofs and august windows that stretched out until lost in the countryside.

The small white clouds over the hills, far away, beyond the pottery, did not stay still for long: they stirred in an instant, billowing out and then galloping quickly away, towards the boundless remainder of the world. He wanted to get home and had to move. He climbed back down the great wall and stopped at the river that frothed around the rock pools of that hostile stretch, now even blacker. He shuddered and jumped quickly across to join the others.

He told them what he had found but was soon jeered for his enthusiasm and especially for his ignorance. More than the others he was laughed at by a young boy from the houses in a disreputable district further down the via Flaminia, almost in the country-side. He was a small, ginger, twelve-year-old, all bone, with a few scraps of scrawny white flesh here and there, regarded by the group as a runt. Damìn tried to stop him. He began to insult him, threatening him, but the boy carried on jeering and taunting him, coming out with arguments and excuses to make fun of him: words and laughter gushed from his little white lips and brought convincing looks to the faces of the others. Damìn was beside himself with rage.

'Son of a whore,' he exploded almost crying. 'You're the son of a whore,' Damìn repeated with all the pain that it cost him to extract those terrible words, hidden beneath his own truth.

The runt laughed even more, thrusting out his arms, with the white flesh of his chest drawn into two thin slabs, and said simply: 'You are the son of a whore. You're mum's a real whore. Everyone knows it, and everyone says it.'

The clarity of his words made everyone stop; and he began once again to laugh and talk at the same time, describing how a real cunt was made, all the real cunts he'd been able to look at and even touch; since he hadn't always had to spy to see them, but had even been shown them wide open, offered to him between splayed legs, with the pussy slit between the skin, without underpants, from the stomach straight down to the arsehole. Damìn stood there not knowing what to say.

'You are the son of a whore,' he replied automatically. 'You're mum's a real whore. In the houses down there, they're all whores, all the women . . . all the women in the houses down there.'

'Perhaps,' replied the runt. 'But your mum's a whore as well. Your granddad knows it too. Your granddad knows all about it, even if he's forgiven her.'

DAMÌN SANK DEEP INTO THE TRUTH that was now in the open, further magnified by the mention of his grandfather, by his awareness brimming with pity, so generous and flowing that it touched him there and then, in the midst of that pitiless group, heightening his desperation to a point where he was completely lost. The truth that his mother was a whore went beyond his comprehension, it went beyond his universe of truth and pain: it was confirmed first of all at home, leaving no space for the obstinate denials of his affection, and then outside, for everyone and everywhere—in the town of Fossombrone, all its buildings and its people who in all were more than ten thousand.

It was reconfirmed by the runt who turned to Manaccia, the oldest of the group, now over twenty, disabled, retarded and epileptic. He turned to him as if to an impartial judge: 'It's true, no? Everyone knows his mum's a whore, and his granddad knows it too.'

A smile broke across the whole of Manaccia's flat clammy face, a smile broader than the sweat, broader than the whole open collar around his enormous neck, above his chest of thick hair. He nodded in agreement, slowly, with a solemn gesture that culminated in his Adam's apple sinking to the bottom of his throat.

He swallowed the sorrow of having to agree, combined with pity for his good friend, always sad, generous with slices of bread spread with grape jam and with money for the cinema; fourteen cents to get in at the front, in the first rows, and six for the human company of three Popolari cigarettes. When he was able to add one cent of his own, making it seven, he could even increase their supplies by adding a Moresca liquorice to two Popolari.

Manaccia watched Damìn, and his face relaxed once more on account of his pity, fully hoping to see Damìn draw his fists and hurl himself at the runt from the houses at the bottom, who would have avoided him with plenty of ducks and swerves and would have moved in counterattack, with the courage and agility of a country boy, of the fatherless child brought up to fight from the very first plateful of food.

Damìn showed his fists at the end of his taut arms, firm and trembling, apart, rigid as stone beneath the flow of tears. The runt must have realized his opponent had little chance and clambered halfway up from the sand, with a watchful intimation that he would quickly finish him off if he had to.

Damìn remained there with his outstretched arms and fists, clenched and trembling, and mingling ever-more desperate threats and denials with his tears. His tears soon became all-consuming, and the universe of his unhappiness exploded within the sightlessness of his eyes. Damìn put his hands up to his face.

Manaccia stood up and, after another pause, told the runt to clear off. He took Damìn by the shoulders and with a clement hand he pressed his face upward. He held his head firmly, benevolently, in the same way that other good friends had to hold him when he was struck down by the illness he had been born with, on the cobbled street or the gravel.

HE TOOK THE DISTRAUGHT BOY away from the river to the bus station, which seemed the right place to calm him down and distract him, with all the movement, perhaps with the arrival of a convict in chains, wearing a cap on his head and shackled here and there, held by police officers, speaking words of a strange dialect from the South or one of the large faraway cities.

'*Mamma mia*,' said Manaccia. '*Mamma mia. Matre maia*,' he said in a mangled Southern dialect he had picked up once from the red lips of a criminal, one who had murdered with a cut-throat razor.

'*Matre maia*, where have I ended up,' the man had said, dressed in a jacket that was tight and yellow as a mandarin orange in front of the snows of Fossombrone. And he had fallen faint beneath the handcuffs. The police had pulled him onto a chair at the cafe and there he had revived, only to carry on complaining.

'*Matre, matre maia*,' Manaccia now repeated, 'you who gave birth to me like this, who have t-taught me

75

to swear and steal, who have t-taught me to beat my father and b-barter my sister, you who used to go thieving even in ch-church . . . you wouldn't have given birth to me if you'd known in what place you'd imp-prison me. Fossombrone, Fossombrone, you're the tomb for my poor remains. Sad dark tomb filled with black snow and stones. *Matre mia*, you should have carried on being a whore, even into your old age, rather than producing children for a place like this.'

Manaccia was having fun almost singing the words uttered by the convict from the South. At the end he said, in amusement: 'And he didn't even have any socks, when the police stood him in the snow.'

Damìn was almost consoled by the story, formed around the repetition of *Matre maia* which even he could say without the fear and the pain of having to pronounce the word 'Mother', unburdening himself with that strange manner of expressing the real and pressing terms of his own tragedy. *Matre maia* gave him a way of referring to his mother that was still possible, new and even tender. And the horror of the convict, so passionate and melodious from that yellow face, could be well measured by him as an exaggeration in front of the truth of Fossombrone, however intractable. So that in comparison he could regard the horror of his own truth as being relative and disproportionate.

'*Matre maia*,' the two friends repeated together. Manaccia still smiling, his face less clammy, offered Damìn a moretta—coffee with anise and rum—at the tavern along the Corso, near the cinema. He made him drink it down in two gulps, with a brief pause in-between to say how good that moretta was, so famous and much lauded, though certainly not as good as the one his father used to make with bootleg grappa when he came home from the abattoir after slaughtering ten pigs, three sows for Fermignano porchetta, a herd of sheep from Pietralata, five lambs from Fratterosa, a lame horse from some land agent, and hammering open the skulls of fifteen or so cattle, including the low-quality beef brought specially for the prison each fortnight from Forlí or Arezzo. The heads of these beef cattle that arrived from outside, asthmatic and as old as the hills, were always tough: after the first blow with the largest hammer, his father had to break the bones of the skull with a miner's chisel, one of those used for excavating the Furlo tunnels, the only kind that would split ten-thousand-tonne blocks.

Manaccia drank his moretta, sucking it continually between lips pursed in a porcine pout, after which he banged down the glass and turned to Damìn.

He clasped his enormous hands beneath Damìn's jaw in an explosion of affection and said: 'They're all whores in m-my house, even the ch-chairs.'

THAT AFTERNOON DAMÌN RAN DOWN to the sports field and, inventing an excuse, persuaded the attendant to give him a regular-size javelin.

He stood at the edge of the field, brandishing it with a powerful emotion that gradually subsided and evened itself in the poise of the javelin as he held it. The pole began to quiver, building up the energy that spurred him to run and launch it.

On the other side of the field, Marcacci emerged bare-chested; Damìn continued blindly but with a clear-mindedness that brimmed to the fingertips and directed the javelin in the direction of that womanizer. It flew spinning, sailing long through the air over the sports field, curving down and piercing the ground a few metres from its target, on the cinder boundary of the area mostly trampled by soccer players. Marcacci looked at the javelin thrust in the ground, measured the whole arc of its flight with his eye and, taking three steps, he went to pull it out.

'Well done,' he called to the young thrower, 'well done, come here, tell me your name.'

'Well done,' he said once again to Damìn, who was panting in front of him, 'very good, you ought to come and train . . . join the young athletes. What's your name? What school? Where are you from?'

'I'm Damiano Possanza and I'm from Fossombrone, on the Cassero bend, above the river,' proclaimed Damìn, straining as if for another throw.

'Possanza? . . . Possanza the potter?'

'Yes. Grandson of Damiano, son of . . . '

Traiano Marcacci looked him straight in the eye and then broke into a vague, indeterminate half-smile. Damìn took a step forward, decisive, like the combatant in a mythical realm who has to stand before a rival general before competing on enemy soil, and, still following the mechanical movements from *L'Avventuroso*, he retrieved the javelin from the hands of the enemy leader.

He spent the night half-awake, with his hands on the hard pole of his own rudder whenever a notion brought him close to any of his worries, even just one small and marginal aspect of his own reality.

NEXT MORNING AT SCHOOL, between the usual first and second hour with the Italian teacher, the head-master appeared in the uniform of a major in the Bersaglieri, with a wide-brimmed feathered helmet on his brilliantined hair. He studied the wall at the far end with the air of a worried titan and announced that not all of them would make it to secondary school, especially if they wanted to study classics. Not all of them. Just a few, very few, the best, carefully chosen, the future leaders, future builders of the nation and its greatness, of Fascist order in the world, of *pax romana*. Not all of them therefore. Certainly not the fanatics, nor those

sick in body or in mind, nor those who are overly religious, who couldn't then attack their enemy and be
justly, bravely victorious. So not all of them. What do
the *Iliad* and the *Odyssey* teach? Not all could be like
Achilles or Agamemnon, nor even like Ajax, nor even
like Ulysses or Hector: some might be Menelaus. Many
on the other hand will be sailors, archers, foot soldiers,
porters—porters of supplies, of weapons, of vases.

'Vases,' Damìn repeated to himself, 'filled with time
and ruin.'

He left school that day with the idea that he would
start breeding pigeons. And taming them as well, so that
they would fly around freely cooing between the windows and the vegetable garden, over the river, as far as
the woods on the hillside opposite, and return in
excitement with their tails ever wider and brighter.

HALFWAY THROUGH THE AFTERNOON he couldn't
manage any more homework, in front of the window
that overlooked the dull blocks of the outer ramparts
of the town, and ran down to Occhialini's workshop.

'But Italy today, would it win a war against France?'

The discussion went on until evening. An
hour before closing time, two craftsmen came to visit
Amilcare for a chat. One brought two bottles of good
wine to celebrate 28 October 1933, exactly a year from
when a Fascist squad had turned the cobbler out of the

tavern in the piazza as an anarchist and a subversive, not fit to be seen in public premises licensed by the state— by the state and therefore a Fascist license.

Damìn stayed listening to the discussions between the three which, after the first flurry of excitement, proceeded slowly between drinks, or was lost among empty cheer and curses. And they ended up talking about money, poverty and farm labourers.

'Farm labourers are all turning into Fascists,' said one.

'Them, Fascists?' protested Occhialini. 'With their hard work and their poverty? That's inconceivable. Their hard work and their poverty are bound to turn them against Fascism. A true proletarian can never be a Fascist . . . not even if he becomes brother-in-law of the Duce . . . or of Marcacci.'

'A potter, the owner of the pottery and a quarry, is he a proletarian?' Damìn ventured. 'A potter who hasn't studied, who works with his hands, who has always worked, who owns the pottery and the quarry and is also selling at the market, what is he?' he repeated to those who gazed in astonishment.

'Your grandfather's a fine craftsman, almost an artist—even if he hasn't studied. He knows how to work and how to think, with his head and his hands. The finer the craftsman, the more of a free thinker he is—one who supports the proletariat, who understands and helps them. But if he doesn't join with them in the fight, he's on his own, neither fish nor fowl . . . and it turns out badly in the end. Someone pious and idealistic like that could become a Fascist, but certainly not a materialist like your granddad who loves his work and respects the work of others!'

And with this consolation Damìn was offered a beaker of wine like a grownup: it was drinking time.

The three men carried on drinking, evermore silent, reduced now to exchanging smiles and congenial smacking of lips.

One of the two comrades tried to resume the conversation and told how something incredible had happened less than a month ago, though it wasn't widely known. Inside the local Fascist headquarters, halfway up the staircase, under the great picture of Mussolini standing on the Furlo dam, someone had left an enormous piece of shit, at night, in the dark, right under the photo, and into it had stuck a cane stick with a piece of paper on which was written: 'Duce! Here I've done it, and here I'll leave it, not for your Fascists, but all for You.'

All three laughed together, spilling the last wine on the floor. They looked down at the stain. The shit, they said, had been so big that the party secretary had to call the firemen to clear it up; and they described its size: builder's shit, the size of dumplings, of beetroots, of chestnuts, of butter beans, of new wine.

In their enthusiasm they gave one another a friendly embrace, as far as the workshop door, climbing the two steps with a single leap.

OCCHIALINI WENT BACK to the patch of wine, and studying it again with satisfaction he turned to the boy: 'What fine poetry, honest poetry . . . but you didn't smile much. Why?'

Damìn made no reply, struck by the vulgarity of their bravado, muddled also by the effect of the wine.

'Why?' the cobbler asked again.

'It's not with poo that you fight the Fascists,' said Damìn, giving vent also to his inner feeling of despondency.

'With poo, no, but with shit, yes,' interjected Occhialini. 'Not with poo, but with crap, yes. Crap well made, and well organized. It can change the course of power,' he explained with satisfaction.

'But are you frightened even of shit?' added the cobbler, intensifying his gaze over the redness of the drink. 'Aren't you overdoing the shame? Aren't you frightened even to say these words? All those filthy things said?'

'No, not frightened,' said Damìn. 'It's me who says whore and slut, isn't it? It's you who denies the truth and avoids those words.'

'But you only use those words to condemn. You use them out of fear and hatred, like poison.'

'But a woman who ... who ... ' Damìn was eventually almost shouting, over his own pain like the cobbler over the patch of his spilt wine, 'as well as fucking ... does ... does other things, other filthy .... horrible acts ... then she must be a whore ... and even worse ... a real slut.'

'And why? Not necessarily,' replied Occhialini, climbing back on his chair. 'And why can't a woman enjoy making love, doing all the things to do with love, especially if she's jilted by her husband, especially if she's in love. All acts of love are natural, even those so-called acts against nature. So the woman who falls in love isn't a whore ... '

'Not even if ... not even if ... ' Damìn insisted; and here he had to resort to forms of phrases so frequently used that they no longer contained that aspect of truth that disturbed him, he had to investigate that truth; he was prevented from pronouncing the words themselves for fear they reminded him of those acts, would make him accept them for what they were and even repeat them: ' ... even if she takes it in her mouth ... kisses it ... licks it?'

'No, 'cos she could just be doin' it t' make 't good for 'r man.' And the dialect offered him much easier forms of expression. 'You love a woman, she's never a whore. Never! Not even if she takes it up the ass, never, not if it's love. A whore takes money, and that's that—like when she makes love for a second fuck. And then don't forget, a hard cock's always good . . . and's never bad for anyone, least of all a woman in love.'

Damìn kept silent but certainly gave no sign of acceptance. Occhialini realized it was time to close shop but, still feeling the need to offer some instruction to the boy who was still there beside him, he continued: 'I believe the soul actually exists. The proof of its existence is garbage—garbage in all its forms and in its varied smells: that's the evidence of it. Or rather, the soul exists because garbage exists. Otherwise, where would people find so many evil ready-made and ready-numbered thoughts, and such a capacity to harm themselves and others?

'Science, revolution must serve to cancel out the traces and the position that such garbage has accumulated over history, through religion, through superstition. Start yourself off like that.

'Never take anything as cut and dried—especially following current opinion and the view of ignorant people and hotheads. You have to study, to read. What about *Les Misérables* by Victor Hugo, *Oliver Twist* by Dickens? Or *L'Assommoir* by Emile Zola or *The Mother* by Gorky? Why don't you go down to Pesaro some time to hear *La Traviata*? That at least was written by an Italian.

'Climb out of that vase of yours, Damìn, it's time.

'Do as your granddad does—he makes his own vases, makes them as he chooses, then he has them sent off, sells them.'

Damìn had mixed feelings, stung with pain and anger at the word 'Mother', and the word *traviata*, fallen woman, while the example of his grandfather brought him hope.

HE SAID GOODBYE TO OCCHIALINI, judging him to be drunk; nonetheless he had a lingering suspicion that behind that freethinking cunning there was a real truth, about people, places, events; and that this truth indeed intimately affected him, in what was happening, and in time—as in the fire of awareness, of breath. The sun was in the evening sky and the moon already high at that hour, revealing every detail of the walls of the streets as he walked down to his home: surely they were trying to show him how clearly Occhialini was fooling him, with his story and his questioning; and the phosphorescent traces of the snails and the cobwebs also revealed just how slippery and alluring the cobbler's net could be, thrown out to catch him.

At home with his head still whirling, he found several pots fresh from the kiln at the far end of the corridor; they still held the aroma of their firing and the enveloping light of the glaze. He could see they had been made by his grandfather, and with particular care. He bent over them, touched them and paused to listen to the distinctive voice of each that reverberated alone or at the strokes of his palms.

After supper he went early to bed, with the idea that he would start making and firing pots as soon as he left school, and would become a free thinker, capable of acting alone against everything and fighting against injustice. He roamed in the uncertainty of whether or not his own sorrows, plans and anxieties could be regarded as ideas and whether or not he was an idealist, destined therefore to become a Fascist and a leader. Then he held himself tight and grasping his dick he drifted away.

VI

The Love Letter. Blood. Winter.
Breast-Feeding

NEXT DAY IN CLASS, Jenner, his only friend, stood up without the teacher's permission and announced he was leaving school as his whole family was emigrating to Argentina, where they'd been called by an old relation of his mother.

'What's your father's job?' asked the teacher.

'Does manual work . . . odd jobs, from labouring to hod-carrying to farmhand.'

'Ah! Good, well done. Best of luck. Have a safe journey, best wishes to the new world.'

Pretty Cerignola put up her hand and asked to go to the toilet. Jenner watched her leave in amazement and remained standing longer than necessary: then he bent over the desk with his legs half-out, like someone who no longer had any concern about the school and its rules, and began writing a note. He sat down to fold it, still staring at the girls' desks, and kept hold of it until the last bell. The girls left first, in orderly fashion, while he stayed where he was at the far end, holding the note. He watched the other faces with nods and goodbyes.

Outside the school's main door he still had the note in his hand. He kept looking around instead of going straight to the bar on the opposite corner where four of them usually waited to catch the train home. As the pupils were leaving, he saw Possanza and called across to him.

'Hey, Possanza, hey, Damìn. And just to think my granddad always told me if I didn't do well at school he'd send me to work at Possanza's pottery . . . Do me a favour, give this note to Cerignola tomorrow. Don't let her see you, and don't say a word. When I get back from Argentina with a pile of cash, I'll buy you a motorcycle.'

Damìn was thrilled by the errand and by the secret, and spent the whole afternoon at the cinema next to Vitina; but even in that atmosphere of distraction, every now and then he would finger the pocket containing his friend's message. In bed, that night, he opened the note and read it.

'Dear Nicoletta, I'm sorry to be going if only because I won't see you again. I love you. I don't think much of books and films. But if I actually come back rich then I'll search you out all over Italy. I don't know if you've ever felt any love for me, but I'd really have given you my blood. Please don't forget me now, so I still have hope. I hug you and kiss you on the mouth and all over. Farewell. Farewell youth. Yours, Jenner Ligustri.'

Afterwards, more lonely and guilty than ever, Damìn masturbated for consolation and to overcome the feelings that had swept over him with so many traces of an external truth that should never have entered his bed.

Next morning he reread the note and found its writing to be very modest, almost ordinary, though sincere. Its sincerity touched him and kept him embarrassed over the word 'blood', without too much mixing of semantics, nor even allowing Jenner to think up phrases that were more original and more suited to a repertory of love.

'FAREWELL YOUTH' WAS JENNER'S CONCLUSION on his departure. Damìn couldn't avoid the comparison, wondering therefore what point his own youth had reached. Throughout the morning at school his thoughts became caught along this line, forcing him to think about himself. Everything was marked out for him, in and beyond his youth. Unlike the boy at the bottom of the class, he didn't even have the spontaneity, the obligation, the thrill of leaving Fossombrone.

He looked down at the shoes, the clothes, the wrists, the hands, the knees that held his pain together, so that his pain could continue to exist and survive. He ripped up the note and stuffed the fragments into his right pocket under his handkerchief. His left pocket had a hole in it so that he could always reach down to his dick, his ever-present and mysterious companion, always there to feel and hold so that it wouldn't disappear.

Outside school he threw the scraps of Jenner's note into the pile of litter behind the newsstand.

It was still only Wednesday, and there were two whole days before *L'Avventuroso* appeared. At that hour the pigeons had all lined up under the eaves of the town hall. The sky of Fossombrone was distant, with a ridge of clearer cloud that ended on the other side. The outline of the hills and mountains rose on its own account, on both sides, with crags and rocks. The Romans had tunnelled at each end so as to enter and leave the valley and its plain. The Duce's Alfa Romeo drove past at the strangest hours, never stopping, throwing up stones and wearing holes on the bends. Forum Sempronii. Fossombrone . . . 'Fossombrone is a town / Accurs'd to all around / My aunt lives there as well / and she's accurs'd as hell.'

DEATH HELPS CHILDREN GROW UP to appreciate the older members of the family around them; it helps them understand life, mortality and the naturalness of its course.

They watch the old person they love grow sick and waste away, closed up in his own world; and then they see his dead corpse. And meanwhile, through grief, they begin to understand the rules of existence and mortality. Death assumes a connection with time and with reality—so alien to them at their young age, and for bodies like theirs.

Damìn didn't have this experience. The first old person to die in his family, his grandmother, was involved in a car accident while she was by herself, outside the house, carrying a basket of vegetables, knocked down one evening on the via Flaminia by a racing driver in the Mille Miglia who was testing out the route. Her body was taken to the hospital mortuary and from there, once identified by Damìn's grandfather and the legal formalities were complete, straight to the cemetery without being viewed by any other members of the family, due to the horror of the injuries.

Damìn remembered that smell of death and its rituals, the sapping, nauseous scent of strange large flowers that wilted and dropped their petals onto the fresh wood of the coffin. This too gave off its own smell, of nails and planed wood. He had a desperate fear of treading on the petals and stems that dropped from the hearse right beneath his feet.

After the funeral the whole family gathered around the table, for coffee, and carried on doing so at regular intervals for the rest of the day and through the next.

This gathering around the table to remember his grandmother became a new custom, though various matters of business had to be discussed because of her death. The racing driver who had knocked her over was a somewhat eccentric aristocrat from Perugia: he had no insurance and would have to be sued for damages, which Dorino considered entirely appropriate from a moral point of view.

Onorati, the lawyer, had asked for a not-insubstantial sum to be deposited as an advance on necessary expenses.

DAMIANO POSSANZA PREFERRED not to pay out and not to sue; all the more so since it looked as though the racing driver of noble blood didn't have a lira to his name.

'That's what you think,' protested Dorino. 'All the flowers he sent for the funeral alone must have cost him at least three hundred lire.'

'I don't want to destroy any of my work, nor squander it, nor let anyone else make use of it,' Damìn's grandfather had said; not least because two days earlier he had been examining the business, and prospects for next season.

'And I don't want to destroy it either—least of all what we have achieved, you and I. But you think of work simply as work, of what you do with your hands.

And you think of production as a row of so many vases, jugs and pots all neat and tidy, which bring satisfaction and admiration. I, on the other hand, think about the benefits of work and the results—what we get out of it, and perhaps what we could get of it by working less. For example, buying and selling products and industrially ready-made crockery. And not just earthenware but also china, aluminium, enamelled tin, steel. People no longer take jugs down to the spring to get water, they don't just cook in copper pans over the fire, or in earthenware pots on the stove. Many now have water in the house and cookers with bottled gas. And then, wasn't it you who never wanted to do decorative majolica? Never to depart from traditional models, colours, sizes? Never to make fancy pots, ornaments . . . ceramic sculptures?'

'That's right. Fake artistry has always been the ruin of those who've produced it—first because they get big ideas about being artists, ceramicists, sculptors.'

'And so? We carry on with our pots, and in much larger quantities, so long as they're cheap. But at the same time we introduce new products, more in tune with the times, more popular . . . Otherwise we run the risk of others muscling onto our patch.'

'Let them come. I want to see who can make pots like ours. And if someone can make them as well as us, or better, then he'd have good reason to come forward and take the prize.'

'But if the winter stops us for six months and if the market is changing as it is? Those who don't move forward in business are soon overtaken.'

'He who stops is lost!' said Possanza ironically.

'And if that were true? And if everything really is changing, the whole of Italy, work, business, industry under Mussolini's great projects? Land reclamation, new cities, asphalt roads, housing projects, schools, sports, transport, hospitals . . . '

'Military barracks . . . '

'Yes, even barracks. Would it be such a bad idea for us, for we Italians to go to Africa or Asia to win a colony, to open up new fields of work?'

THE MAGNITUDE OF SUCH A PREDICTION brought silence. Damìn's mother came and asked him quietly whether there was a love poem in his anthology of literature. Damìn was taken by surprise and didn't answer; his mother moved closer and asked whether there was a poem with words of malediction . . . over a broken love. He didn't know what to say and went to fetch the book. He remained there as his mother searched, page by page. She found nothing suitable so she asked for the Italian dictionary.

Damìn stayed by his mother as she anxiously searched for the words love, affection, promise, betrayal, beseech. She showed no embarrassment and as she read and reread the words with her lips, made notes on a piece of paper or tried writing whole words and whole phrases with the correct spelling. At the top of another sheet of paper she wrote in fine letters: my dearest. She paused and thought for a long time, with her pen still poised over the paper, but wrote no more. She returned the books to her son, tore up all the sheets of paper except the last, which she folded and tucked into her left sleeve. Then she went to her room. Damìn carried on gazing at the door she had closed behind her, seized by a strange optimism.

The door reopened and his mother came back, saying winter was destroying everything. She paced around the dining table and in a measured tone said: 'It destroys and throws away.' She went to the window overlooking the garden and continued: 'It's not true that winter encloses and conserves. It destroys and throws away. Cancels. Especially in a town like this, on the river.'

Desperation must have made her talk like this, aloud and alone, while the two men of the family were in conversation.

Many times over the next few days Damìn found her writing at the kitchen table, at the dining table, on the flat surface of the sewing machine and even at the dressing table in her room. She had two or three sheets now, and various words written here and there as notes pleas. The letter was not progressing, while the woman's anxiety increased. She also tried to go out, sometimes on unlikely or entirely new pretexts: to talk to her son's teachers, to take Lavinia to the dressmaker, to the hairdresser. And returned still more anxious.

During the hours when she could go out, even on the most unlikely pretexts, Marcacci was closed up inside the town's social club, among its card games and billiard tables. He left when most people were already at supper, around eight, to wander the piazza, to see and, above all, to be seen by the few who were still there and who were generally the town's most influential men.

Damìn understood his mother's plight, and rejoiced and suffered in a way that conflicted and alternated evermore swiftly and profoundly, so that the two feelings, rather than conflicting, were now coexistent and conjoined.

AT THE NEWSSTAND HE BOUGHT what he took for love stories and left them casually on the dining-room table cover, by the edge of the palms of the oasis. Once, browsing among the books faded by the sun on the front row of the newsstand, he found a manual entitled *The Book of Love Letters*. He bought it and read it twice, putting himself alternately in the place of each correspondent, before leaving it where his mother would find it. But he never managed to see the letter she had written, nor discover or intercept other messages.

Winter continued its work of destruction. The fires in the hearth followed swiftly, one after the other, shooting up the chimney with sparks ever larger and more garrulous. Damìn's mother often went to the porch from where she could look up to the town, and stood there, for no purpose or reason, looking around her at the ragged outline of Fossombrone. Or remained behind the closed door, as though absent, and without showing that she was waiting for some footstep or call. At night Damìn often heard her talking quietly with his father.

As Lent approached his father refused to take her to the carnival ball, or to any other festivity. Indeed he criticized her for having asked him, when he should still have been in mourning for Grandma.

ON THE FIRST DAY OF MARCH, when the weather was still bad, she insisted it was time to spring-clean the house for which a daily helper was needed.

The woman who arrived was approaching old age, loud and coarse, better as a gossip than for any domestic chore. Yet she had to rush about following Norma's instructions. After barely three days of her chaotic presence, Traiano Marcacci came knocking at the door.

It was Damìn's mother who opened it and led him to the centre of the room where the uniformed centurion, having declined to sit or accept a glass of wine, made the announcement that had brought him there.

Damìn and his grandfather were standing next to each other by the French window looking onto the garden. Marcacci said he was sorry the person to whom his message was addressed was not present. He brought news that Dorino Possanza's application to join the Fascist Party had been accepted: valid from 1929, from the date of the Duce's speech in Pesaro in defence of the lira, in other words, in defence of the Fascist economy and production, even at the level of small family business. Marcacci spoke with his right hand resting on the table exactly over the orange minaret of the oasis; directly in front of him, the mother's left hand fumbled in the turquoise sky towards the largest star. Damiano Possanza acknowledged Marcacci with a slight nod at the beginning and the end of the visit and remained with his grandson throughout, turning constantly to look at him.

Damìn watched, transfixed by the sight of the woman and the man together, and by their beauty; he delighted in their coolness and nonchalance and meanwhile suffered for the brazen betrayal that was being committed against him, against his grandfather, against the whole family ... the house, the room, the cloth on the table—against all those images that had, as always, at the centre of their film, heavy and unbearable and lingering in the shadows, the guilt of being Norma's son. He burnt with the desire that Marcacci might turn to him, that he might recall that brilliant javelin thrower.

In his grandfather's rigid silence, in the discomfort of the half-turn he made towards him, as if to shield him as the triumphant guest said goodbye, he felt the disappointment, indeed the physical insignificance of not being the one to whom that radiant woman was speaking, the object of that glossy smile on her mouth, constantly nurtured by growing happiness. He would have liked to be the full measure of that gaze blinded by the colour that spread and reverberated over the star-spangled blue of the oasis.

Once Marcacci had left, with a military salute accompanied by the click of his heels, Damìn ran to rummage about in the cupboard as though there was something he had to find straightaway. He wanted to wait for his mother to cast off some of that resplendence that was not for him, some of that excitement she had shown for the enemy, and to regain her impenetrable composure.

With his eyes closed inside the cupboard he pictured her bosom ravaged by his feeding at her breast, her two nipples still bruised by his mouth, and between them the cleavage into which he had buried his hands with an infinite grasp of pleasure and power. He waited for her to reappear resolute and upright, unblemished bastion of affection and health, warmed by a light waft of perfume.

VII

Nobody. 'Una furtiva lacrima'.
The Passing of Geese. A Heap of Infamy

ON THE FIRST DAY OF LENT it snowed heavily for four hours after dawn. All the members of the family stood one behind the other in front of the window looking out over the garden to watch the snow. The first to get up had been Grandfather who found its white mantle spread across everything. Soon after, a strong wind began to blow from Furlo which made the snow and the whole valley tremble. The snow gathered in the corners exposing the riverbanks and the fields; it clung to the tree trunks and the edges of the walls. In the garden it swirled about for a long while covering the space with a frothy swirl; then when the wind dropped it appeared curly and light on the plants and the herbs in the garden. Its white embroidery shone uncertainly, more prominent and compact, against the damp blackness of the objects.

Damìn, who always loved snow, compared it to the embroideries on his mother's dressing gown, those on the collar and around the cuffs.

The garden, decorated in this way, no longer bore the marks of his mother's passage and her betrayals. The same nightdress appeared whiter and neater, buttoned up well over her body to conceal its guilt. It had become a garment of penitence.

The snow glared at the blackness, and in the young boy's mind it reflected a hope of atonement and change. Its wisps stood as the sign of a possible miracle, one that was already taking place. And so, before going to school, he wanted to accompany his mother to church to the Ash Wednesday rites.

Together they trampled the blanket of snow that was crisp beneath their feet. Every sound and voice rose shrill into the dense air and fell immediately with a brief hiss. The snow had opened up another dimension, where everything appeared smaller and safer: the footprints they left, as well as the opposite flank of the church. It was all purer, thought Damìn, so much so that he was looking forward to taking the sacraments. He made his confession keeping to the more usual set phrases, which yet had the effect of freeing him, and he took Communion with a conviction accompanied by an infinity of tastes.

His mother, however, was breathing heavily with lips parted in expectation of the host; her eyes wandered here and there as if to ward off some unwelcome discovery. Her neck was bare and feminine, more ardent than pious.

A young novice sang Gounod's 'Ave Maria' with a fine full voice.

Damìn followed him with delight but was gradually drawn towards an awareness of absolute purity that he and his mother had not only lost for ever but hadn't ever dreamt of.

Before the singing ended he went to wait in the sacristy among the church's young servers whom he knew. One of these dressed in a long surplice was sermonizing to the others:

At midnight comes the watch
And people scratch their crotch. Amen.
At one o'clock the missus
Goes outside and pisses. Amen.
At two make love with a pauper.
At three with the king's daughter.

Together they divided up what was left of the hosts and star-shaped candleholders. They rattled the offertory boxes and rang the bells in the courtyard. Then they threw themselves onto the girls who were leaving, and hugged them and fondled them with the excuse of sprinkling ash over their heads. Then they surrounded one of them and wouldn't let her go.

Back in the sacristy, Damìn heard the novice who had sung talking to a man from Fossombrone and reassuring him he had now learnt the whole of 'Una furtiva lacrima' and many other arias from the same opera.

'If only I could get permission to go out,' he heard him sigh.

Meanwhile Damìn's mother was lingering in the darkness of a side chapel with an intention that didn't seem one of devotion and certainly gave her little solace.

' "Una furtiva lacrima," ' said Damìn. 'Those merry young girls,' he added and thought about that group, that enthusiastic throng of girls he would never meet— and least of all share their gaiety. The snow outside had almost gone: all that remained were a few capricious flakes, almost scorning their precarious destiny, on the leaves of the evergreens and on the bars of the railings.

At the end of the street, a small procession of mourners was crossing from the dark doorway of the hospital mortuary, carrying a yellow pine coffin on their shoulders.

'Who has died?' asked someone nearby.

'No one,' replied a man at the door of a shop that sold threads and buttons halfway down the street. 'Just a farmhand.'

The town walls grew gradually darker and narrower towards the via Flaminia, whose sounds could be heard higher up. They were replaced now by the sounds of a steamroller and many pickaxes, pulling up the old stone road to make ready for the asphalt, and cutting away a sharp bend in front of Passionei's stables.

IT WAS HERE ON THIS BEND during the first afternoons
of the school year that Damìn and the children from
the districts on either side of the main road used to wait
for the farm carts that came to the wine cellar opposite
with crates of freshly picked grapes. Each farm worker
would steer the oxen in front and every so often, if he
was alone, would look back at the cart and its load, and
protect them with a long whip. But the children managed almost always to clamber up behind, appearing all
of a sudden from behind the wall on the bend, stealing
from the crates, even if they were covered with pieces
of sacking. All of them would succeed with impunity,
happily laden with bunches of grapes. Damìn was the
only one who had difficulty: he'd time it wrongly, getting to the back of the cart too slowly or too fast, and
be seen each time. A farmer hand had once had a go at
him with the whip and struck him right across both
shoulders. The blow caught him full-on and the mark
of the rope cut right into the skin. The others laughed
at him, but he lied, pretending he had missed the blow,
or at least hadn't felt it.

Perhaps it was the same farm worker they were
now carrying away in that yellow pine coffin. He felt a
touch of emotion, and sent him a sincere and affection-
ate thought, shedding several tears in spite of the cold.

Further on he saw two boys from the sacristy who
approached him and demanded money and cigarettes,

offering him candle stubs and, more importantly, promises of protection in exchange. Why should he have to be protected by others? What did other people know or think about his situation? When it came to physical strength, he could have beaten all three of them at once, able as he was at his age to lift a hundred-kilo sack and carry it on his back for fifty metres at least.

At school he thought of nothing else but tests of strength and endurance. He could have resisted even if they tortured him with a flaming sword. The whip of that poor farm worker had been nothing to him. And yet that peasant had been smarter and quicker than he, with those poor unripe grapes, all stalk, from the Cesana hills—with a cart that seemed more like a rough sledge than wheeled transport.

At home he threw himself greedily on his food, shunning any conversation. He ate as much as he could, neither appreciating nor enjoying it, thinking only of filling himself to get strong.

The cinema was closed and *L'Avventuroso* was now several days old and no longer had anything new for him.

He spent the afternoon looking at the ruined tower, trying to focus his thoughts on the wall, trying to make it collapse. He thought he had actually managed to shift two or three bricks in one of the chinks.

Then he turned his attention to the valley, to its voice and to how it changed along the course of the river.

SUDDENLY HE REMEMBERED an event about which he had chanced to received news and ran towards the ser-vicemen's dance hall, where the musical instruments were still propped against the stage and where the novice, accompanied at the piano, was to sing 'Una furtiva lacrima' for his patrons and admirers.

He listened to the song from behind the door, even more beautiful when heard from a distance: all three times, as many as the young friar needed to satisfy the enthusiasm of his audience. Some of them urged him at the end to sing the song about Sacco and Vanzetti, but the novice refused, blushing, afraid of infringing the Fascist ban on it.

It was dark by the time Damìn got back home. His grandfather was at the front door and greeted him enthusiastically: 'Stop, stop,' he said. 'Hark,' and he pointed up at the black, black sky. Little by little Damìn heard high up a sound, distant and sorrowful, of birds drifting, chilly, insistent and plaintive.

'Listen,' said his grandfather, pressing him by the hand, 'a flock of geese coming down from the Apennines towards the valley, chased by bad weather. They're calling to one another, but they won't lose their way. They're going down to Calcinelli and the lake at Tavernelle.

They're flying down in a V—the most experienced one leads the way and cuts the air.'

Damìn was touched by the call that repeated itself and spread as it moved away, but touched even more by the tenderness of his grandfather, so good and innocent, a master so full of generosity towards animals, and to all the things of the world.

Fossombrone had lights along the streets and at the corners of the eaves for those returning home alone and with no guidance. Many lights switched off and many others broken; and many homes unhappy beneath the three hundred and eighty-three tiled roofs that made up the town, plus the other forty-one roofs of stone, plus the nine terraces that covered the new homes built for wounded servicemen.

AT THE END OF LENT, when the voice of the fireplace was much fainter while that of the river had grown, climbing the walls and the branches of the trees up to the windows, the night encounters between Damìn's mother and Marcacci began again. They were suffused above all by the woman's tears and supplications. She held on to him, calling his name, pleading, beseeching, and even when they lay down to make love, she never stopped sighing and imploring.

After the fourth of these meetings, on the morning of Palm Sunday, the woman who had been taken on to do the cleaning appeared early at the house. She was demanding something in a loud and evermore insistent voice, pressing Damìn's mother into the corner of the kitchen between the window and the sink—like a prisoner, to judge from the muffled noises that reached him in his room, which must have been made by her hurried movements to defend herself and escape. After two more desperate and confused sounds, Damìn could hear his grandfather's footsteps across the dining room, halting at the doorway to the kitchen. Then he heard his voice, deeper and firmer than ever.

'What do you want here, you old troublemaker? Who's given you the right to come in here accusing and complaining? I'll throw you out with these bare hands, unless you leave fast. Come on, say it aloud, say whatever you have to say! Say it out loud. Tell me the great, shameful truth . . . tell me . . . and I'll laugh even louder, in your face and in the faces of all those like you—those throughout the town, if the whole town's as vicious as you. So tell me this woman has a lover. Tell me who it is, and how many times she's seen him. Well, what do you think? That we would turn her out for this? Or for one of your nasty ideas we would damn her and punish her for ever? Get out, get out while it's clear to go . . . and take your heap of infamy with you. I can tell you and all your townful of hypocrites that she's a poor woman who has fallen in love. She's incapable of hiding anything, in what she does, in how she acts—because she's honest, because she's open and because she's not like your race of bigots and liars.'

The woman must have left in a hurry and without a single word because right after these words Damìn could hear his mother sobbing, her cries whirling round and round as though she couldn't find a way of letting them out. She moved dishes and bottles, opened and closed drawers, shut the window, pulled the curtains as she continued to cry. His grandfather must still have been there, in the same place where he had spoken. Damìn heard him turn to go back to his room. He heard him shut the door in the usual way, with two distinct clicks. Could his mother now ever meet Marcacci again?

VIII

*Boots. Rhetoric. He Drives through the Whole of
Italy. The Lacquer*

SHORTLY AFTER HE REOPENED in the afternoon, a
woman arrived at Occhialini's workshop holding a
pair of men's boots; she entered ceremoniously and
stumbled, ending almost on top of the cobbler. She
lifted the boots high, one in each hand, and announced:
'These belong to Commandant Marcacci. He would
like them slightly darker, more brown. And the heel on
the left to be widened.'

Occhialini was taken aback on seeing the pair of
boots above his head.

'Ayah! Ayayah! You don't say!' he exclaimed, almost
singing. 'The boots of a squad leader, a truncheon
wielder, one of the very first . . . a true, fearless saviour
of the fatherland.'

'Yes, yes,' continued the woman, 'and make sure
you do it well and fast, with a decent lacquer, one that
doesn't burn the uppers.'

'But are these really Marcacci's?' continued Amilcare
merrily, as he took the boots by the heels, allowing them

to flop, lowering them meanwhile from the mighty height at which the woman had displayed them. 'Which Marcacci?'

'The commandant,' repeated the woman, 'Traiano Marcacci, an important man, Fascist leader.'

'Which family?'

'Son of the late Doctor Tarquinio Marcacci and Signora Adriana the schoolmistress.'

'Ah, yes, yes. Signora Adriana . . . She was my teacher,' admitted Occhialini. 'I remember her well . . . ask her whether she remembers Tufty . . . they called me that because I always had two tufts of hair sticking out over my ears and because I used to sit there quietly and still, eyes wide open. My grandma used to cut my hair—she was half-blind, and worried quite rightly about snipping my ears. I used to keep quiet, eyes open, to learn everything. I knew that was my school, the only good thing I might ever be given, and I had to learn as much as I could to defend myself as best I could.'

'Her son is the commandant. Make sure you do a good job, to keep Traiano happy. He's so meticulous, so unpredictable. When he's in a bad mood it means trouble for everyone. He's so overworked, full of thoughts and worries . . . about everything, everyone . . . about his responsibility, about the public good.'

'Have no fear, such a pillar of society will be served as is due. And his boots . . . . colour, heel. But did he know you were bringing them here, to me?'

'No, no. The signora told me: go to Occhialini, down the Scalette del Giro. He's the best . . . Her son was there too, but didn't say anything . . . '

'Very well then. It's up to us, we ourselves, to put the commandant back on his feet, indeed back onto his pedestal. We'll perform this social duty swiftly and satisfactorily. Come back at midday tomorrow.'

When the woman had gone, Occhialini took the boots, once again by the heel, and showed them to his young friends and disciples.

'These boots!' he proclaimed, 'the silliest footwear worn by men. So much leather and sole, used just to display the arrogance of those who wear them—their military, authoritarian spirit . . . spurning everyone around . . . wherever they set foot, wherever they trample, protected and blind up to the knee. And then just the same up the tube of their legging right to the top, to the head of . . . With this stupid tube of hard leather, which itself seems the monument to Fascism, its emptiness and its blackness, its yen to reach everywhere and seize everything.'

'These boots are soft,' he continued, 'for the countryside, the colonies, yellow for the reason that they're colonial, or for the landowner at harvest and threshing time . . . soft, for the well-dressed adventurer, explorer, horse rider. Not for parades . . . that's clear from the colour, but for work, for manoeuvres—fine work and fine manoeuvres . . . Who knows why he wants them darker!'

'So as not to be seen at night,' said one boy; and Damìn had immediately thought the same, seeing the stout boots with which Marcacci went to the nocturnal appointment with his mother.

'Maybe,' replied Occhialini. 'But I reckon it's more accurate to think he wants to tone them in with some uniform, for some procession or parade. The boot is typical footwear for parades, pointless as much as vain, with the heel reinforced to make more of a noise when marching, and to be more sure of an effect when he clicks them to the orders of his superiors and true masters. Boots are authoritarian and servile, exactly as befits our so-called ruling class. They are also bad for those who wear them . . . for the instep and for blood circulation, for the calf and for the whole leg. But he, the great leader, isn't bothered since they are worth the sacrifice. And perhaps he doesn't even notice, involved as he is in the parade. And then as footwear they are uneconomic, unhygienic and smelly . . . and if a scorpion or a viper gets inside you certainly won't get them off before you're bitten.

'They don't keep out water, nor snow, and you can't walk in mud without slipping over, not to mention ice. . . And they stay cold in winter and hot in summer. And the coldness and the heat continues to rise inside, to the point when each boot tightens and you can't get it off—it sticks to the leg, suffocates with it. No labourer, no farm worker, no miner, no blacksmith, no carpenter, not even a woodcutter has ever worn a pair of boots. They'd prefer to go around barefoot, or in wooden clogs. Nor have true soldiers ever worn them—only noble horsemen, and then officers . . . Never trust anyone who wears boots. He's certainly not an honest man, but always one who feels different and superior to others. Hannibal didn't wear boots and nor did Hasdrubal at his last battle here on the river Metauro. Ah, if he had won,' pondered Amilcare, now carried away by his epic of self-learning as a rebel and a communist, by his determination to do good and to make others understand, methodically knocking in a tack wherever one sole ought to be in relation to another, even in the margins most covered and least concerned about the holding power of its new formation. And he almost sang, talking over a wave of notes and even in the evocation of his readings of poetry, of social and popular poetry, inflated and accompanied by an assembly, a march, a movement of protesters or workers. 'Ah, if only they had won. Maybe having blacks in Rome would have been better than the whole arrogant white race of princes and stupid pious Christians. Napoleon wore boots, and yet . . . But Nelson wore a pair of socks and ordinary light shoes, all hand-stitched without even a hobnail. Mussolini, bourgeois reformist and socialist, sham revolutionary, he wears boots . . . all the time . . . as if he'd been born in his boots. He even has boots in his throat, in his voice . . . his words echo like they're inside the tube of a boot . . . his gestures are mechanical, irascible, just like someone standing in boots that are pinching . . . and who doesn't want to take them off, frightened of losing authority . . . and even of letting his feet be seen . . . the white feet of the bourgeois son of a schoolmistress or the forked hoof of the reactionary demon. No surprise he drives his car so badly . . . that each time he drives past he destroys a parapet or knocks down a road worker . . . He's gouged the whole of the Furlo tunnel with his mudguards, maybe trying to dig through just like the Romans, and every time he passes here on the via Flaminia he churns up the road and even wears holes in the stone, with his sudden, rash, booted manoeuvres . . . He passes through the town like a foreign body, boot on the pedal . . . not looking. He's never cast his eyes on the castle or deigned to look at the cathedral or the bell tower or the buildings in the town. He has never noted the houses . . . the doors, the lights or the shops. He heads towards groups of people, straight as his boots, sloughing into them for the fun of watching how they jump against the wall, out of his path. He drives through the whole of Italy like this: the commander, the commander under the command of his boots. In Russia they wore boots, yes, even the revolutionaries and the farm workers; but there they are made of felt, short and light, specially made for the snow and the mud of the steppe. But if anyone went there with a pair of boots, even as soft as these, he would get nowhere, nowhere at all, not least because the people's tribunals would have him arrested right away—they'd take his boots and send him off to work, to labour for the soviet, for the collective good . . . And that's if it goes well, for the boot wearer, for the bourgeois and militarist agent—because he'd run into a patrol of red guards who, as soon as they see those tubes on his feet, would shoot him on the spot, leaving him half stuck in the mud, dead and still standing in his boots.'

The cobbler had started painting the lacquer over Marcacci's boots, dipping a small brush into a square bottle and then rubbing it in with his hands. Despite his contempt for them, he worked the boots well; he fondled them and warmed them with his breath to dry the lacquer. In the end, whenever he worked, his skill and knowledge as a craftsman always prevailed.

The lacquer bottle gave out a pungent odour that caught the nostrils and was rather like the smell of the cinema when it first opened at two o'clock on a Saturday afternoon, after being closed up from Friday.

Damìn sniffed the smell and, following the bottle with satisfaction, he watched as Occhialini replaced the top and noted where he went to put it back.

IX

Regional Championships. Group Prize

At six in the morning the piazza was empty. It had been built sideways between the town hall and the other buildings, and stretched not quite as far as their walls and the stairways to each of them. In the higher corner, conspicuous beneath the sun, was Marcacci, dressed all in white, with a wide jacket that flapped tightly around various points of his body with an infinity of creases, belts, buttonholes and pockets. The bus was due to arrive with athletes from Urbino and would collect Damìn and two five- and ten-thousand-metre runners from Fossombrone. Marcacci would be in charge of the whole group, including those who got on at Fano, and would be one of the judges at the regional championships in Ancona.

It was the first time Damìn was going off alone, leaving his family and the town; though as soon as the door of the bus had closed, and as he headed towards the games, he was comforted by the thought that he was under the command of Marcacci, the man who had brought ruin to his family and distanced him from the town; and who was now protecting him and was to be his guide and judge on his first journey into the outside world.

Damìn and the two runners approached Marcacci who sized them up and greeted them. He looked at the bags they were holding and berated them:

'You imagine the Fascio will let you go hungry? You are ignorant and suspicious, like peasants, whereas you should be athletes; you are serving your fatherland, not going on a pilgrimage to some religious sanctuary. This is a bad start . . . get rid of those bags; away in the rubbish. You might have brought some spare socks instead, or white shorts; I don't want to see you competing in your underpants . . . '

The older runner protested: 'I've got my shorts and socks in there. The paper's greasy because it came from another bag.'

'Me too,' continued the second runner, 'I've got my shoes in it.'

Damìn couldn't find a way of lying and looked around for somewhere to throw his bag.

'Keep it,' said Marcacci, 'keep it. You can have it this time, keep your homemade omelette—you're still juniors.'

Damìn was even more confused and stared at the braids on Marcacci's uniform. He followed them in their downward cascade, studying the whole of his body: his slim waist, lost immediately, like a hollow, inside the great black belly, closed here and there by the strips of his side pockets, and then the straight crease of his trousers.

The bus arrived and the three filed on behind the leader; first Damìn and then the other two who kept a careful distance from the person in charge. Marcacci settled himself in the front seat and ordered Damìn to sit behind him in the second. Marcacci stood up as soon as the bus had left, and turned towards the group: 'I'm in charge. You'll do as I say. You know I want to win, and therefore you have to win, no choice. For me and for our local Fascio. You have to give it all you've got, spit blood. You have to beat the teams from Pesaro and Ancona. You don't have their training, but you're not sissies either, not like those who spend their days strolling about the city.'

'They go to the brothel,' muttered one stocky youth, a hammer thrower from Urbino.

The bus sped along and the wind fanned Marcacci's curls between his ears and collar. Damìn stared at him and saw the dark curve of his cheek, the shadow of his cheekbone almost blue. The smoke from his cigarette wafted into his face and every so often a tassel of his uniform flapped back, onto the metal of the seat where Damìn was sitting. Close by he felt the weight of that body that was the obscene object of his mother's love. He would have liked to see it better, to touch it. Even to injure it.

Through the fixture of his gaze, barely breathing under that smoke, Damìn felt sick, and vomited.

'By God!' shouted Marcacci, as he felt splashes on the hand he had placed on the other side of the back-rest. But then he took care of Damìn, told him to take deep breaths and close his eyes. He told the bus to stop and made him get out for a walk and some fresh air. At Senigallia he made him gulp down a Fernet. Damìn was feeling ill but almost relieved that his sickness had stopped him from continually watching Marcacci, consumed with hatred but also fascinated by the sublime qualities of his figure. His nausea kept him in his sandals, clutching his knees trying to make sense of the grim signs inflicted upon him by his life and by his age.

In Ancona, once off the bus, Marcacci bought everyone a cappuccino and told them to do three push-ups before and after drinking it. The sea shimmered inside the port, right below the city, and gave off an animal aroma.

On the sports field each answered when called, and they were organized and separated by category. Almost all the javelin throwers were from Ancona and Pesaro, elegant and preening. Damìn watched the group of runners who fortunately weren't far away, and at the edge of which, well separated, he could see the two from Fossombrone, still with their bags. On the journey they had continued eating from them, and drinking.

When called for the competition they simply removed their trousers and ran in their underpants, with the shoes they had worn before.

Marcacci was with the other commandants, conspicuous among them by reason of his height and his uniform, which continued to flutter like a flag even though the air in the stadium was quite heavy. Damìn was sweating, having barely recovered from his sickness. He tried to find some shade where he could wait, sitting on the ground with his face resting on his knees. He could feel once more the traces of his scars. When he looked up he felt bewildered and always ended up searching out Marcacci. At the sound of the bugle all the athletes had to stand in line. A band of marines played the Fascist anthem 'Giovinezza' and the Royal March. Once the music had stopped Marcacci stepped forward, climbed onto the platform and, with a megaphone that reflected the light of the sea, read out the Fascist Oath. Everyone yelled: 'I swear!'

Damìn too, at the top of his voice.

'POSSANZA,' HE HEARD CALLED, and he arrived at the appropriate position, not even removing his jersey: he had to take it off there, and left it by the chalk strip that marked the line. He threw well but, one after the other, his throws were disallowed. Each time, his foot had crossed the line.

He was to be disqualified, and the judge was already approaching to inform him when Marcacci arrived. He took the judge aside, said something in his ear, and stood next to him in the position of arbiter, swollen with the authority and status of his position.

The judge called once again: 'Possanza! Possanza, get ready for the last attempt.'

Marcacci approached Damìn with an apprehensive smile and muttered: 'Take your vest off. And just for once, don't disappoint your mother.' Then he resumed his position of authority and went back to fluttering, with arms crossed, beside the judge. He too repeated: 'Possanza to throw.'

Damìn went to take up his position, his head tilting more than the javelin; he measured out a very long run up, graduating his breath as the pole, little by little, evened itself in his grip and, twenty centimetres from the enemy line, he hurled the javelin, crumpling his whole self, until his bitterness brimmed over. The javelin went straight in its direction and flight, and sped not too high over the field, way across, to vanish from sight at the far end against the line of the metal boundary fence. Its point arched down towards the track on the other side and finally stuck in just before the red earth. It was accompanied during the final stretch by the roar of the crowd, which suddenly fell silent as it veered down and struck the ground. After another instant, a burst of thunderous applause. Damìn was still crumpled within his own bitterness, his eyes lost behind the lance of his defiance. In his bewilderment he heard the applause and looked at Marcacci; he saw him jubilant, his arms raised high. The throw had been forty-eight metres, a top mark even for the seniors, incredible for a junior: a regional, perhaps a national record.

Marcacci came up and hugged him. Damìn was rigid, but after a moment he yielded and buried his face among the tassels and the stripes of his uniform, against his shoulder. Marcacci's scent was strong and confident. Damìn absorbed it, conscious of not feeling the repulsion he would have expected.

FROM THEN AND THROUGHOUT the day he was the centre of much attention, from the Pesaro and Ancona players as well. The regional team coach asked him about the way he trained. Damìn smiled without answering. By throwing stones, he thought a moment later; all the stones I've thrown against everything: river, water, bridges, streetlamps, vegetable plots, trees, dogs, lorries, cars; by throwing stones, he thought again, and started searching for a stone in the sand and cinder track. Throwing stones had taken up whole days, complete seasons of his life. Throwing stones instead of jerking off, to avoid it, and to forget it. Stones thrown at targets, as signs or omens ... if I get that far ... if I hit that ...

Later, just after one o'clock, they all went to eat at
the district military canteen, served by girls in Fascist
uniforms.

The two runners at the centre of the table had two
helpings of everything, and drank endless amounts of
wine. Damìn was invited to the judge's table, next to
Marcacci, and was too nervous and shy to eat and
frightened he might not use the right cutlery. He drank
mostly mineral water. To overcome his feeling of bewilderment, he asked to go and sit with the two runners.

'Not bad, eh,' they both said, 'not bad . . . all for free
. . . even the girls . . . just gotta get 'em to bed now . . .
forget the running.'

'But we'll run,' said the ten-thousand-metre runner. 'Hell if we'll run. Gotta get back for an eyeful o'
this at least one more time.'

In the afternoon, none of the javelin throwers, not
even the seniors, reached Damìn's mark, increasing his
triumph even more. Marcacci stood with him, displaying
him to everyone: authorities, journalists, athletes, sup-
porters. Both of the runners from Fossombrone arrived
in second place, just beaten at the end. 'They had
nothing left in them,' said Marcacci, 'no style, no proper
training.' They went back to their bags and sat on them,
pallid, with their tongues out. Second in the region,
top-class, well-seasoned runners with no style, with no
training and no shoes, with their best clothes now

strewn crumpled and splayed on the grass. They sat down, not bothering to limber down or to do any breathing or stretching exercises like all the other useless athletes around who were more exhausted than they were.

Marcacci came back and said, almost menacingly: 'You're no athletes, you can't pace yourselves. You don't even want to win. You're no more than peasants. You don't have the urge, that second wind that makes you a winner. It'd be a waste of time bringing you here again.'

The two looked at each other and a smirk came across their faces. One muttered for both of them: 'Urge. Urge t' run with them . . . let 'em win. It's our pricks wot 'ave the urge . . . just you see what urge!'

The older one lit a cigarette and hurled himself almost violently onto his back in the grass. The other stood and went off to look for some lemonade and to get closer to the group of girls in shorts.

Once the competition was over they all gathered by the bus, worn out and with nothing more to say. One of them called Felice, a boy from Urbino with a broad cheerful face, had won the pentathlon; but only two others, apart from the three from Fossombrone, had managed respectable results.

'Let's go and see Ancona,' said the pentathlon champion, but the others yelled at him and began laughing. They were all set on the same idea, expressed forcefully and aggressively by the hammer thrower from Urbino, as if he were swearing: 'Let's go to the brothel,' he said, turning to Marcacci. 'Take us to the brothel, Commandant. After the sweat, the reward. That's the motto of the Fascist workers' club.'

'All right,' replied Marcacci, 'but you each have to pay for yourselves.'

There was general applause and the bus drove off towards the alleyways by the port.

When they arrived in front of the small dark-green door through which could be seen a second door of frosted glass, Marcacci counted everyone again. The only one missing was the fencer, a young marquis who had stayed behind, sweating in his white silk shirt, in his seat at the back of the bus. Marcacci looked at Damìn and gave him a nod: 'We'll wait outside, at the cafe just here.'

Then he turned to the others and announced: 'No more than half an hour.'

DAMÌN SAT IN FRONT OF MARCACCI at a small marble and metal table. The man looked at him, and Damìn felt himself yielding to a shame worse than if he had gone into the brothel. The man himself, the whole of him, disturbed Damìn more even than the memory of the encounters and what Marcacci had done with his mother: he felt exposed, moved by a propensity that overwhelmed his recollections and his feeling of bitterness. Marcacci bought him an aranciata, poured it, handed him the glass and his own handkerchief to wipe his lips. He too was embarrassed enough to start offering his own suggestions and advice on how to improve Damìn's skill in javelin throwing.

'You have incredible shoulder-power . . . a long muscular arm. You could become national champion, go to the Olympics, play for Italy. You have to carry on, Possanza. I'll talk to your parents, and your teachers too.'

The others did indeed come back after half an hour, and started knocking back liquors: triple dry, double kümmel, cherry liqueur and then shared a round of Vov. The two from Fossombrone ordered wine and mixed it with lemonade. They came from the country, sons of farmhands and building labourers. They ran because they had always run, from the time they learnt to walk, from home and back, for errands or just to get away. They had been spotted by members of the Fascio at a cross-country race during the Sant'Ippolito village festa and had been signed up on the junior athletics team.

Marcacci took the same seat on the return journey, and Damìn too, having declined to sit next to the centurion. Everyone behind was talking about the brothel: some had found her tight and warm, others wide, some black and covered in hair, some blond velvety and fair;

some had been attentive, some sullen and lippy. Some had just fucked without hearing or seeing a thing. The older runner was still going on about hairs that were long and black, and a tongue as slender and agile as a snake. The younger one laughed, nodding at everything, his hand held over his face with two fingers up.

At Fano everyone got out and drank another toast to the Fano players. Later, back on the bus, Marcacci sat down beside Damìn. The others had stretched out to sleep. The two from Fossombrone were still rummaging among their bundles of food. Damìn remembered he had left his on the washbasin in the changing room on the field. He felt homesick and moved further away from Marcacci, to his side of the seat. Marcacci was smoking with his head raised, and looked down just to wind his watch, a large sports chronometer full of hands and dials. He realized it was no longer going, swore, took it off his wrist and slipped it into his pocket, brushing Damìn's bare leg with his hand. He buttoned the collar of his jacket now that it was night, lit another of his Serraglio cigarettes, turned and smiled at young Possanza, regional champion. He was his lucky prize, his regional, perhaps his national hope.

Damìn wondered whether Marcacci was thinking about his mother, and in what way, with that smile and those teeth, with that pungent smoke that stung his eyes. As he grew tired it seemed as though this proximity might make him guilty of putting her into his mind, might make him guilty of acquiescence. He grew tense again and, using the excuse that the window was too draughty, asked to go and sit further back.

Leaving Marcacci by himself, he sighed and relaxed against the seat, now that the lights of Fossombrone were flashing one by one against the windshield of the bus. 'Here, we're back,' he thought, 'another face in the piazza at Fossombrone, in this . . . eagle's nest, valley of pious conformists, pisshole of priests, marketplace for bourgeoisie and bailiffs . . . O Fossombrone, imperial ruin . . . '

In the piazza at that time of night, Marcacci offered to accompany Damìn home, no longer with the authority of a commandant; but Damìn gave him the slip and found himself alone on the cobbled street, above its rocks, then hurried down the slope towards the walls on the river.

The brown front door of his house brought to mind the shiny green door of the brothel in Ancona. And if he had gone in? And why had Marcacci stayed outside to keep him company? What did it mean? That Marcacci could now tell his mother everything? Or that he had genuinely preferred to remain with him, to keep guard over his precious champion?

He thought of the two runners who were certainly still thinking about the hair and the tongue as they ran home through the rough dark lanes of Sant'Ippolito.

He remembered he was regional champion and, to soften the impact of being back home, he remembered his freedom, and his gratitude for all the stones he'd thrown, and his new glory. His mother hardly questioned him, but fumbled between words and silence as though there was something she wanted to know but couldn't ask. Damìn gave few answers, not even mentioning, out of deliberate, gleeful spite, that he had won a spectacular victory.

His mother was wrapped in her dressing gown, fortunately well buttoned up, without the frills, cutwork or lace of the dressing gowns worn, so he had heard, by the whores in the brothel. Damìn went up to his room and stopped to look at Vitina who slept, white and pure, motionless, her hair neatly tied, her breath slightly moistening her waxen nostrils.

He could confide his victory to her, without even waking her—all his greatness. That he had won away from home, and away from Fossombrone, and against Marcacci and against everyone else of his kind, all those ambitious, tall, handsome, citizens: the many, even from Pesaro and Ancona, muscular and hirsute, trained and massaged, with silk shorts . . . and enormous dark cocks and balls. His own dick then began to grow hard, thinking about the hair and the tongue encountered and crossed by the two runners.

X

Fascists in the Brothel. Her Tongue and Hair.
The Man of Troy. The Sewer Rat

NEXT DAY HE DESCRIBED EVERYTHING to Occhialini: about the day out, the great organization, his victory, and the final reward at the brothel, describing the group's expedition as though he too had taken part, not so much to boast as to avoid admitting he had remained alone with Marcacci.

'So you had a go, then?' asked Occhialini. 'You had a look, at least? You liked her? Was she nice? How was she?'

'Dark,' he replied, 'and hair like this.' And he pointed to his hand and halfway up his arm.

'A southerner. The Abruzzo?'

'No. I don't know. Her tongue was as long as a . . . '

'Her tongue? You saw her tongue? She stuck it out? To do what? With one like you who certainly doesn't need to be licked about, and was certainly frightened of kissing her.'

'But I did kiss her!' he lied again, trying to remember the others' stories.

'And to kiss her you saw her tongue? You'd have felt it.'

'Yes.'

'Clever boy, well done. Did you say anything? Ask her anything? Where she was from, what she thought, what she liked, how she began?'

'No. No words. She was sighing.'

'But she didn't say anything? She's the first brothel whore in the world who doesn't talk! Wasn't she even rude to you? Perhaps she had a headache. And what did the others do? The valiant athletes . . . Fascist conquerors . . . in the brothel . . . always in the brothel. And the great Marcacci? He as well, which whore did he choose? He'd certainly have chosen first, he, the leader. And he'd certainly have chosen a blond, refined, foreign type.'

'No,' and Damìn, through his lies, felt an ever greater urge to defend his leader. 'No, he didn't go in. The whores wanted him, they were looking for him— but he didn't go in. Or rather, at some point he went out, waited for us outside.'

'So then. He, the handsome conqueror, is outside. He doesn't need the brothel now, the centurion!'

These words, to Damìn, seemed to trespass once again upon his truth, so he tried to change the subject.

'He's a real leader. Down there in Ancona everyone respected him, and they listened to him on everything.

The organization, the lunch—such a nice place, with good food, plenty for everyone. Chosen and prepared just for the games—light and nourishing, with fruit drinks and mineral water. Doctors and nurses there and ready all the time. Emergency services, ambulances, Red Cross women. And then the showers, towels, tracksuits, shoes for field and track, some with toecaps depending on the event. All perfect, well arranged and carried out—one game after the other, judges, measurements, timed with stopwatches, the awards ceremony, scoreboards, team lists, all really good, the whole region, with different badges on their jerseys, equipment, instructors . . . '

'Yes, and then the brothel. First the military display, the parade . . . the athletes ready like soldiers, lined up, trained and ready always to obey. And then the brothel, the usual reward, the usual outlet for the submissive . . . the usual fuck, to get their own back, like tyrants . . . which doesn't help people to live freely, for sure: it has nothing to do with true love, with respect.'

'What respect?' asked Damìn, his truth once again touched.

'Respect for oneself and for others, for women as well. Especially women who offer themselves and pay the price.'

'But aren't women glad to give it? Isn't that what you always said? Don't they also want it . . . all of it?'

'Yes, but not those in the brothel. They are there for the money, they are bought and sold. What choice do they have? In the end their tongues really can be like a snake that slithers around without ever saying a word. They no longer have any freedom, they're exploited.'

'But there've always been brothels. Even before the Fascists.'

'Of course. Otherwise, how would Fascism have begun? That's exactly where it started, in that practice of domination and disdain, of compassion and exploitation, of impotence and braggadocio. In any event, you won. And you've had your first fuck. Good, that's a good thing at your age. Though it would have been better if you'd done it with a girl from school . . . a girl you loved . . . who had followed you willingly along the river . . . and you'd stripped half-naked—there together, both for the first time, trying together to work out how it's done. But still . . . better if you've fucked, better than jerking off . . . if it helps you get things straight in your head, over and beyond your prick, rather than just thinking and looking . . . just looking and thinking . . . just thinking about it and then making up stories and jerking off.'

He ALTERED HIS TONE and, after a long sigh that made Damìn already feel apprehensive, he was more direct:

'And how are things with you? That business you've been following? Seen those two any more? They still meet under the bridge? What else have they been up to? Is the woman still so worked up, so passionate? Is she more unhappy or getting over it? Is she making the most of it and preparing to forget about him, or getting more sighful? Perhaps she thinks she'll find someone better—less handsome but less selfish, and more solid. Someone who can understand her, help her. You'd see then how she'd suffer less, be less mopish, less prone to melancholy,' and he chuckled and became more playful, as though it were idle chat, 'but more lively and cheerful, more enthusiastic around the house.'

'Now it's you who's talking badly about women,' said Damìn in defence. 'If I told you she was unhappy . . . that's because she really is . . . her husband's weak, he's always away, and she's a good, kind-hearted woman who's fallen in love with a good-looking man, tough but also good, who seems decent, noble—and he is. She's unlucky enough to have fallen for him, in her imaginings, in her kindness. In her beauty, so beautiful and loving even in her hatred, in her tears, in her hair, in her clothes. It's a secret love, but it's real.' He managed to transform anger into pride, resentment into pity. 'Poor unhappy woman, she can stir pity, but not disgust . . . full of guilt, so much guilt, but innocent . . . The woman cannot choose, nor change, nor run away—she can only sin . . . and suffer. She feels regret and pain more than pleasure at her cruel, fond sin.'

'Yes. Yes, well done, I'm pleased you understand her and you're defending her. Good, that's how it should be. I hope you mean it . . . ' He paused and continued slowly, his voice firm, ' . . . that you're not denying the real truth so that you don't have to endure it and suffer. It would be worse to hide, and worse still to cover it up badly, bottle it up. Certainly better simply to under-stand what love is—love that is also physical and has all its needs and satisfactions. You've talked about this woman now with affection, like someone you know. Like someone perhaps prevented from making love—love denied and indeed unthinkable . . . immaterial, like for some . . . yes, for some kind of nun.'

Occhialini managed to correct himself in the end. He felt an urge to teach but also to challenge this boy who that morning had praised Fascism rather as though he were a Fascist himself. And he had no wish to hold back in his tone or in his words, which were indiscreet and offensive, which as well as being persua-sive brought pain—a salutary pain for that boy, in his blindness and bitterness about family and school, already attracted towards Fascism, captivated by sport and by organization.

DAMÌN'S PAIN WAS TERRIBLE INDEED, even stronger than if Occhialini had said straight out that he'd understood it involved his mother—his mother and Marcacci, both lovers and Fascists, both caught up in the pleasure of sin and enjoyment, for ever and against everyone, deliberately against everyone: children, family, town, general order, reputation, respect, decency, innocence, the constrictions of society. She a whore, more a whore than those in the brothel, she being neither poor nor for sale; but a whore in spirit and in flesh, a traitor, betrayer of affections in the house, its rooms, its beds, in the daytime, in her children's upbringing; a betrayer and squanderer of her children's love, of their innocence, or their age. Damìn said no more and soon left the workshop; he walked up towards the square and the newsstand and remembered how the previous day another commandant had jokingly called Marcacci 'Troiano' with a laugh and a wink.

They knew in Ancona as well? They knew in the same way as Occhialini knew; how he wished everyone knew about this damned communist cobbler—spreading around his stories, his pain, his atrocious, vicious words. Even in Ancona, instead of Traiano they were calling him *Troiano*, with double meaning and malicious complicity. Troiano, lover of a *troia*, a whore, that whore who was his mother.

His pain was transformed once again into bitterness against his mother the *troia*, the whore: it was so bitter and so great that it seeped from him like water and breath, becoming uncontainable, impossible to fully comprehend and certainly to accept. He then had to stop and move away . . . and he fell back on that mouse of a cobbler, on that black rat discharged from the hospital sewer into the river—that sly and vicious subversive who had been playing around with him, who had deceived him, who had pretended to be sympathetic and even to help him understand. For the sole purpose of finding out more, of plundering and exploiting the whole of his truth.

The truth, in the hands of the cobbler, became even more filthy, packed with so many lurid words and deeds, with all the most unnatural and indecent details of intercourse. Occhialini became the moving force, the perpetrator, as if it were he who had made these things happen through his questioning and his encouragement.

Occhialini must be taking pleasure in his pain and so became worse than Marcacci who was taking pleasure in his mother, who was mixing his hard, cruel prick with something that his mother didn't even have, that she didn't need to have. Occhialini was certainly worse than she was, ruining herself for love, swept away by the spilt honey of her body and by her predestination as an outsider; by her destiny to marry Damìn's father early and quickly because her family had fallen on hard times, no longer able to keep and look after her until she was an adult, until she could find the true love of an officer, of a gentleman from Rome or from Bologna, or of a doctor at the hospital.

Damìn's suffering made him remember even more. His mother had told him how she had spent over a month in hospital in Urbino as a young girl, and how she had fallen in love with the doctor who was treating her, a distinguished man of over sixty whose whole face was smothered by a white beard, and how happy she was when he bent over to hear her cough and his beard filled the whole of her bed.

Occhialini! Occhialini! Greasy, shaggy-haired, mean and prying observer as his surname suggests, with the guile of a monkey he had deceived and betrayed him: hurt more than betrayed, had dragged and abandoned him in his pain . . . Like a leather sole, glued and fixed in the vice to transform it by artificial destiny into something new, something that is then passed on to others; worn down by daily use, of the lowest and filthiest kind, constantly, until it becomes useless and is thrown away. Thrown away anywhere, provided it's somewhere dirty and dark.

Behind the alternatives of pain and bitterness, he began to glimpse a trail of vengeance, the prospects of revenge.

'Occhialini, you're a rat. And the only thing to do is take you and treat you as one. And I'm already working out how to trap you. I'm already building it . . . the trap that's just right for you.'

XI

The Trap. O acontistés. *The Dictionary*

FOR THE WHOLE EVENING and much of the night, Damìn could cope with his anxiety without even masturbating, thinking up his trap for Occhialini: its mechanism, its bait, its operation, even the spring that would set it off, catching him with no way out. Then someone else would push him under the water tap, until he drowned and burst open.

By morning his plan was as clear, as well-laid as the metal wire of a snare. He went straight to Occhialini and tackled him out loud, asking where he could buy a pair of training shoes, what was the best make, and roughly how much he'd have to pay. Occhialini didn't know how to answer; he knew that he himself had no advice to give the boy, whose voice was so tough and ruthless, so pressing and sad that he stooped down beneath his table to search among his samples of brands and stocks of designs. He could find nothing and re-emerged with only a smile. But Damìn had meanwhile managed to do what he had wanted, taking the bottle of lacquer from the bench. He paused for a moment in front of Occhialini's smile but when he saw that his friendliness meant nothing and would bring nothing, he said goodbye and ran off.

He returned home and put the bottle into a box of marbles that he still kept. The box resounded with the clumsy and insistent note that had so often accompanied the years of his childhood. Those bright yet sombre sounds, that clinked together filling his whole surroundings, marking even the cadence of his mind, had signalled the end of the disconsolate tears of his infancy and then the whole time his sister had suckled at their mother's breast.

The red-and-blue box, full of sweets, pencils and tapes, had been a gift from his grandfather, the only person in the house to care about his tears. The marbles of those years, of the first games with his friends along the town wall, lay there still shiny but abandoned; the lacquer bottle was placed in the middle of their dark and distinct forms, marking a detachment from those times, the square, deliberate order of his new age.

He had matured much, almost abruptly with his determination for revenge, so that the dark parallelepiped full of chemical liquid had become an instrument and was no longer a toy.

He spent the rest of the day in the garden, over the earth and the bushes, catching and swatting bees and wasps. Behind the flowerbeds he went searching in every shape for signs of an appropriate alphabet. Meanwhile he thought word by word, and in each single stroke of every individual letter, about the phrases he would write on the walls of via Gian Francesco Guerrieri and on the parapet at the first bend of the via Flaminia.

'Down with the Duce, puppet of the bourgeoisie.'

'Down with the Duce, ruin of Italy.'

But they didn't seem sufficiently grave and ruinous.

In bed he had no difficulty stopping himself from masturbating and from falling asleep. All the objects around him, even the furniture, were calmly and consciously united with him. The silhouette of light from the window was there to illuminate his plan, and tapered itself so that it could come inside to help, to set his mind at rest in accordance with his decision.

When the light had altered for the fourth time, Damìn felt it was the moment to get up and carry out his plan for revenge. He went into the garden, climbed the magnolia branches onto the wall and leapt down to the steps on the Cassero bend. He ran as far as via Guerrieri, trying to mimic the style of the two runners, and there in the darkness of the night, on the office wall of the lawyer, the father of a girl in his class, using Occhialini's lacquer he painted the first phrase in block capitals.

It came out well, somewhat shaky and slanting, exactly as though written by someone not well educated. He walked straight up to the via Flaminia, to the wall on the corner. There on the stones, avoiding the gaps of earth, he wrote the second phrase, with an excitement that prevented him finding weightier words. There was still a little lacquer left, and in larger letters he could add 'Death to Fascism'.

He found it hard to resist the urge to write 'Death to Marcacci'. But he had to admit that Occhialini would never have been so direct, that he would never have lowered his contempt to the level of provincial bullies, or his class hatred to personal vendetta. He left the lacquer bottle on the ground, went straight down the steps of the old wall, topped with barbed wire to stop people climbing it, and dropped almost onto the roof of his house.

He could see the three steps to the front door when he paused to catch his breath. His head pleasantly absorbed the smell of the lacquer still fresh on his hands. He followed the usual route to his bed in the new room he had been given over the staircase. He felt a long lingering excitement, self-satisfaction, while the ray of light broadened and brightened around him. At dawn he turned on his side to give himself some sleep.

A little after, suddenly waking, still quivering with satisfaction for his deed and anticipation of its outcome, he got ready for school.

NOTHING HAD CHANGED, apart from the light on the steps and over the whole road. But by the bend at the top he witnessed Occhialini's arrest by a trio of Fascists led by Marcacci.

They were yelling at Occhialini and calling him murderer. They had seized him by his arms and his head and were hauling him out of his workshop, his apron still not properly tied. Half-dressed, he was being struck over his naked back and ribs with punches and cudgels. Marcacci was holding up his head with both hands tight around his neck, calling him traitor. From that position the cobbler's gaze, drawn away from the struggle and the strokes of terror, caught sight of Damìn passing against the wall in front. His gaze softened and almost melted on recognizing his friend, but then grew more insistent as if pleading for help or for some flash of indignation. Damìn could offer no consolation and edged along the wall, feeling his way with his hands over the protuberances that he knew one by one. His heart pounded against the wall, and he could no longer feel his chest or his arms, while a taste of vomit brewed in his mouth.

AT SCHOOL, THE HEADMASTER was by the classroom door, dressed in the full uniform of a Bersaglieri major, his hat and his hair shinier than ever, waiting to congratulate Damìn on his record javelin throw.

'A regional, perhaps a national record. They're waiting for further news and confirmation. The emulation of Homer, classical fervour poured into noble Latin blood. *O acontistés* ... this is what a javelin thrower is called in Greek. *O acontistés*, which also means thrower of darts, of glances, of desires ... of ourselves. Here is our great *acontistés*. I remember also your fine essay on the Duce—somewhat fantastical but not without its vision, its intuition, appropriate for transforming, improving ... an all-Italian gift. Your essay too was a fervent outpouring of spear-carrying love, of a soldier ready and committed to face the challenge. What a magnificent surprise ... noble Latin blood.'

Possanza blood, Damìn thought: dense, infused with many things other than nobility ... the lowly blood of potters, the blend of earth and mud. Occhialini's face was bleeding while Damìn hadn't even deigned to look at him: blood was trickling red and clear from his swarthy skin and flowing straight from the light in many thin rivulets, like that of an animal.

With his friends at the river, Damìn had slowly tortured mice and lizards, snakes, toads and hedgehogs, and once even a dog, with extreme skill and delight; and he well knew how, at a certain moment, the blood appeared, materialized ... how at the high point of fear and pain it appears red and clear, shiny to look at, and how then, shortly after, once all semblance and evidence is gone, it would welter into bruises and congealed clots over the injuries and the torn flesh.

He sat down at his desk thinking of the day when he would throw the javelin beyond seventy metres, a world record. He put his hand in his left pocket and with his fingers through the appropriate hole he reached for his dick once again: the usual little cock that grew into a hard pole, haft and rod of surging blood, inaccessible in any other way.

Furiously he kept whole, and distinct from the totality of his masturbation, his mother's gushing blood: in small hollows strewn across that female body which had to be denied.

OVER THE CHRISTMAS PERIOD his mother had started going out in the afternoon to visit a woman she had befriended, whom she often saw at church and at the haberdashery, and who, like her, happened to be from Urbino.

At the woman's house, as Damìn had soon managed to discover, Marcacci was waiting. The lovers had found a convenient place for the winter. The woman had been persuaded to become the compliant procuress through Marcacci's blandishments and rewards and above all his promises concerning the probability of a pension following her husband's death during the course of his employment. It needed the influence of someone in authority to establish the cause of his unfortunate demise: it had to be proved that her husband's pneumonia had been contracted along the via Flaminia, a state highway, where he was working as assistant roadman along the stretch to Furlo, the dampest and iciest section between the rocky gorges of the river, with all the mist that hung there, made worse by the hydroelectric dam. On a mid-January night of heavy ice he had had to remain on duty, right through until dawn, at the mouth of a channel at the point most exposed to draughts from the valley, to guard against bombs and attacks in the expectation that His Excellency the head of the Fascist government, Benito Mussolini, the Duce, would be passing through.

The roadman's widow let them have her own marital bed since she had no other, nor did she have enough sheets and blankets to make up any other convenient place to lie, let alone for two people.

Damìn arranged to do his homework at the house of a classmate, one of his admirers, a sports fanatic who lived directly opposite the widow. But not even there from the balcony could he see anything behind the blinds, which were always shut, whether or not the lights in the rooms were on. He saw Marcacci go straight in through the front door under the portico, and soon after he saw his mother crossing the same threshold from one side, head down, from the darkness of the arches.

After the first wave of fury, Damìn sat dazed in front of his open books, then said goodbye to his friend and went out into the street waiting, moment by moment, for the whole duration of their encounter, for the two to leave. At first he paced up and down under the portico, then ran two or three times nonstop between the cathedral steps and the clock tower. He was holding a pile of books divided under his two arms and forgot them in his clenched hands, as though they had become a part of his own pain. He fixed his gaze on a cobblestone where fossil shells could be seen, or on the cracks between one stone and another. He kept a constant eye on the town clock and the bells: one by one he gazed at the white statues on the cathedral that he tried stubbornly to identify in their rough features, inflated by indifference and cruelty, even by a sneer of contempt for him. More trusty seemed the black stone horse over the porch of the town hall, returning head down, riderless, to announce that the battle for the town's freedom had been lost along the river, at the first Apennine ford.

Damìn also kept an eye on the pigeons that scratched about between the cobbled street and the piazza and lingered in their iridescent, doctoral collars, in their priestly and magisterial cooing, and their hysterical cries when they raised the shit-smeared coral of their claws. It was his grandfather who had once made the comparison between pigeons that wander about cooing and the plump pomposity of the doctoral classes. His grandfather who at that hour was working away innocently and unaware, to keep them all, including his mother and father. His father as well, who went around risking and losing money on the markets even beyond the province, incapable of working as a potter, of digging clay and pounding it, more interested in aluminium, in industrial blast furnaces: that flat sidelong head perforated with hair that seemed too shiny and bristling, just like a slotted spoon.

'Only a slotted spoon can be made with metal and using presses,' his grandfather had said. 'Clay has never been any good for skimming the fat off broth, not even in ancient times. They didn't throw anything away in those days, they never skimmed the fat; and in those days good housewives could even skim the inside of the cooking pot with their fingers.'

'Good housewives,' Damìn repeated to himself. Meanwhile someone was skimming something else, was pounding quite another clay at the widow's house, and was using scoops and metals much harder than aluminium, and more heavily than mechanical presses. His father was muddling along, eagerly and awkwardly, with aluminium, and by handling and turning it in every way he would end up with his fingers cut.

ONE AFTERNOON HIS CLASSMATE SUGGESTED spying on his own mother through the key hole when she had gone to the bathroom. Damìn was stunned by the suggestion, and even more so when his friend explained that he often tried to peer at his mother naked and felt no guilt or fear, but a great thrill, much greater even than when he saw other women younger and prettier. Damìn was curious about these confessions and found in them another reason for his own difference and his own shortcomings. If he went into his mother's room or into the toilet after her, he felt an urge to search out signs of his mother's guilt, of the ever-active corruption of her body that enveloped everything with warm but invisible lather, with revulsion even to the point of suffocation. The image of his mother's most intimate nakedness was confused within an immense, impossible chasm full of folds, laces and wool, certainly the opposite of a figure that might arouse his excitement. The very beauty of his mother Norma, of the young wife renowned along the whole Metauro Valley, could be recognized by him only as a negation of the material body and all its requirements—as a subject of superior, luminous propriety, to be recognized and treated with respect, to be understood only through the purity of filial affection and love.

He had always envied friends whose mothers were short and ugly, and had always imagined them to be happy; and he had often found that their fortune was even greater, in that they were soon freed of the presence or proximity of a father, or indeed had never had one.

ONE AFTERNOON DARKER THAN THE OTHERS, in that grim month of February, he saw his mother hurrying distraught from the widow's house soon after she had arrived, so that he was almost caught by surprise, still waiting at the door beneath the first archway of the portico. Hidden behind a pillar Damìn saw his mother crying with a handkerchief to her mouth. He followed her home, where she entered even more distraught, having lost all control. She might even have met her husband, back from one of his unlikely fairs, and almost certainly her daughter who would have been upset to see her in such floods of tears.

When he went inside he could hear his mother sobbing in her room. Vitina with her hands on the panes of the French window told him that Mama was ill.

Mama had no supper, she didn't appear and didn't stop sobbing. Their grandfather prepared the meal with the help of Vitina whose busy little hands were stiff and white, having been so long against the cold glass of the window. They ate those kinds of ready-cooked food bought in the shops that everyone generally liked, that offered some relief from the family routine. They mixed everything with a round white cabbage that Granddad had gone out to pick and cut, among the last in the vegetable plot. All three relaxed, as though they had forgotten their mother's anguish and couldn't hear her occasional sobs.

With those louder and more desperate sobs, which seemed to come from far down in her throat, Damìn hoped his mother's sorrows might grow and soon completely overwhelm her: her whole mind, her whole body, the whole of time around her. Her pain and unhappiness would purge her and bring her back to the family, to the subjection and merciful power of their affection—and, above all, of his affection, the affection of her only son.

Next day his mother stayed in her room; nor did she leave for the whole week of Carnival, making it seem her son's hopes were about to be realized.

She re-emerged and left the house for the Lent services, but soon returned as if she hadn't stayed for the whole Benediction, clutching a light-blue envelope of writing paper. Next morning Damìn saw the dictionary was missing from among his books. His mother had started writing once again. She was writing everywhere, shamelessly, the bitter twist of her mouth almost wetting the sheet of tormented paper. But that letter was never finished, even though each day she gradually filled all the tables of the house and the work surfaces with sheets of paper, even the flat area of the sewing machine and several upturned saucepan lids. Instead, news arrived that Marcacci had been disciplined by the authorities and expelled from the Fascist Party. It was even said the party secretary in Pesaro had struck him across the face at the end of a harsh dressing down.

XII

The Centurion's Mother and Father. Flies.
African Diary. The Mess-Tin Full of . . .
The Tricolour Banner. To Rome

MARCACCI PAUSED TO LOOK AT HIS MOTHER who had just been laid out on the bed, her head on pillows, slightly askew, still wearing her hat.

He moved closer to remove the hat that had tilted to one side over her darker hair-covered ear, and sniffed the usual smell of sulphur—a more acrid whiff that chafed his lip and the tip of his nostrils. He removed her hatpin and took off the veil covering the moles on her face, twisting her head towards the window. He cursed that nauseous smell that had repelled him for years; he had never managed to understand where it came from.

The army medical officer from Fano had once been to her bedside when she had been confined there with a sprained foot.

'Digestion,' his comrade doctor had declared. 'Bodily hygiene. Stuffy surroundings,' he said, surveying the large black Renaissance-style furnishings and what little could be seen of the faded damask upholstery beneath and between the curios of stuffed animals, mementos of his father's busy career, first as animal castrator and then as veterinary physician, always alongside his more glorious and trophy-laden pursuit as a hunter.

His father had worked ten years as an animal castrator after all his forebears, for more than a hundred years, had held the post of Fossombrone's veterinary physician. But in Urbino he had failed his school final exams three times.

On the third occasion he had managed to seduce a fearsome Latin and Greek teacher from Bologna, a woman of fifty with large boobs, a bust as tight as the via Flaminia between the curves of the Furlo Gorge, famous for her brilliance and severity in all the schools of the realm. He, a whiskered provincial Don Juan, had begun to seduce her during the oral exam, encouraged by the notion that she had been throwing him certain double entendres about Greek and Latin poets who sang the beauty of worldly life, the happy solidity of feelings, and the pleasure of female company, especially that of a shapely young girl. He had grabbed hold of her while she was alone in the secretary's office writing her reports; she had been thrown onto the headmaster's couch and abruptly penetrated without him even undoing her corset or taking off her silk panties, which glistened even when, for a second time, he had tried to tear them off.

Then realizing between her sighs that she was resisting, he had stripped off half her clothing, broken eight whale bones, dishevelled her imperial matronly bun of hair tied neatly between her ears and neck over the real pearls of her earrings, which he seized and pulled off. With a single yank he turned her over on the couch and took her from behind, like an animal, doggy-style. He even tried to force open that tight dark-petalled carnation he glimpsed between the tight folds of her panties.

'We in Fossombrone have opened tunnels even between the buttocks of the mountains,' he had said. In truth he couldn't be sure exactly where he had entered the second time.

He realized he couldn't manage there and then to mount her a third time. So he went to the adjoining toilet reserved for teaching staff and took a mass of paper and a giant chamber pot left there as a wise precaution against some bodily dysfunction of the said staff, or of one or more classes, perhaps of a whole distraught and terror-struck department: it was of majolica decorated with flowers, certainly not from the kilns of Fossombrone, nor from Fratterosa or Vergineto. He added a glass contraption and rubber enema tubes, a rubber syringe for other kinds of washing, a piston pump that had ended up there but must have been part of the equipment and apparatus in the science laboratories, and arranged all of them over the teacher's groaning, splayed and rumpled body.

Meanwhile he invited her to purge herself regularly and to go frequently to the lavatory, now that her sphincteral barriers had been forced open and channelled right as far as the liver and the rectal canal straightened as far as her stomach.

The whole story ended there and then, at least for the private candidate who was failed for the third and final time.

AND SO HE ENDED UP CASTRATING ANIMALS, the last of the Marcacci vets, a line of animal saviours second only to divine providence, to worldly fortune, and to the miracles of Saint Anthony, the shy saint, a peasant despite his merry ways and his whole demeanour, with his round pink bare toes on cord sandals, the pearly splendour of his big toenail, large and radiant as a shaving mirror, protruding there beneath his cassock, an inch above the rough and squalid filth of the ground; while he, with the whiteness of his beard flowing over his whole stomach, up to his clear, spotless bony skull, the rosary; and with the circle of his halo, true noon-hour of the luminous zenith of peasants, of a whole civilization whose hoe-blades, whose heavy long spades with their trusty oak handles shine even through the mist and the mud and the heavy rains of November.

Tarquinio, the proud animal castrator, though having no great expertise, as well as being lazy, brusque and arrogant.

One day, at the town's literary circle, an exclusive domain for aristocrats and landowners, he had been presented, along with the town's other professionals, to His Excellency the Prefect of Pesaro who had come for an official visit, partly out of courtesy and partly to inspect certain account books of the charitable foundations (the alms hospital and the poorhouse). He had successfully amused him, entertained him, won him over and sidetracked his investigation; he had managed (in the general gaiety) to seduce his wife and sister-in-law who had accompanied him, and then to take him back happy and content to Pesaro, to his flat above the prefect's office in the provincial government headquarters, policed and administered by ten or more young Neapolitan officials chosen for their ability to sing, to play the mandolin, clean and cook fish, make pizzas, tell jokes, iron and starch collars, mend uniforms and be ever cheerful, loyal, subservient, etc. etc.

THE TOWN'S LAWYERS AND ITS NOTARY, wishing to thank and reward that charming and alluring ambassador of all the virtues of Fossombrone, concocted a degree in veterinary science for him, with a respectable mark of 105 out of 110, awarded for his discussion of

a thesis on a particular cattle disease found in the middle and upper Metauro Valley, requiring him merely to
leave the town every now and then, following the
timetable and ways of a young student, first at the
Pesaro high school and then at the University of
Camerino, all for no more than two short and carefree
years, from May to November and November to June.

Just two years later, this triumph was crowned by
Doctor Tarquinio Marcacci, veterinary physician, being
appointed by the Royal Italian Army to oversee the
transport of mules and packhorses to Africa in the war
against the Turks for the conquest of Libya.

Down there, between desert battles and rest periods
in the oases, Doctor Marcacci managed to win himself a
bronze medal, partly for his heroic combat and partly for
his skill as a doctor in assuring the good health and readi-
ness of mules to pull a hundred and fourteen carriages-
of-four in the transport of artillery and ammunition
cases, thirty-four horses to be ridden by officers of the
Cavalry Brigade, and fifty or so camels, that being the
approximate number since it was difficult to count
those quadrupeds, among the dunes, with their single
or double humps and with their ruminant tendencies,
so that even when there are only three in a row
they look like at least a hundred . . . all the more, as veterinary physician Lieutenant Marcacci soon understood, for the eyes of a regular non-commissioned

quartermaster from Piemonte, ill-accustomed to inves-
tigating and distinguishing reality due to that habit of
staring among the rice fields, field by field, and then
among the open dormitories of the non-commissioned
officers, the barracks, the districts, the Italian Royal
Army regiments, all the same, wide and empty: in
whose compact, empty greyness the only curve that
can stir him from gazing at the horizon and the plastered compartments is that of the bugle calls, or of the
flies that buzz and whirl around those soldiers confined
to barracks, over their long monotonous hours of sweat
and tobacco, of stinking feet, of lines of foot rags hung
on a wire from cot to cot, of long underpants hanging
stiff, all with the same brown stain in the middle at the
rear, and yellow at the front to the left, rather like a military map and chart in which every sheet represents and
indicates the land to be conquered, an alluring though
unknown continent.

In the desert abstinence to which he was confined
night and day, outside and inside the tent, with the
desert wind or the moon, with jackals or Bedouins,
with or without mail, with or without pay, with or
without intercourse, he too had to trick his sexual
craving; he too, in that nauseous desert privation, with
scorpions and locusts, with the sweet rustling of the
palm trees in the dawn breeze in which he heard a
woman calling, a voice with a Fano accent—the weight

of the large regulation gun, loaded with all six bullets, on his stomach . . . .

His moral outlook prevented him from even thinking of buggering a soldier: a man, blond perhaps, young and fair-skinned and gentle-hearted, like two corporals, one from Genova and the other Venetian; nor of buggering an Arab, a young civilian goatherd nor a camel herder, with a mop of black curls around his fez . . .

The lieutenant himself was then drawn to a mysterious island, oval and hair-covered, with several tender pink beaches strewn with shells and mother-of-pearl. From the time he'd been stationed in that soft but solitary desert, he could no longer throw himself each day onto the softness of a woman. The vision of that island around which he navigated drove him to seek out parts of those maps with his hands, all the more since, as a saving, he had brought regulation underpants. And so he became conscious of the appearance of flies, curious and buzzing, whirling busily nose-up in reconnaissance. At first he tried to follow those bluish insects, identifying one or two of the more colourful and lively ones, to keep them away from his island and from his maps. But these wondrous fliers didn't stray far, always ready to come back to the lower continent, and settle and buzz, chafing feet and wings, on the bridges of his braces, along the road of his belt, on the mountains of trouser

cloth or on the rafts of buttons. At that point
. . . Marcacci connected, in the notes of his experience,
flies, soldiers, islands of cunts, fever, buzzing, masturbation. And he wrote the first inspired essay of his life,
worthy in some ways of the qualification he had gained,
and which is set out here below.

'Flies, the first inhabitants and nymphs of these
brown- and yellow-stained lands; with much recon-
noitring, flights of exploration, landing to collect samples of small tasty plundered flecks, impregnations;
military flies live in the barracks each afternoon through
every season of the year, for decades, for centuries faithful to the filth and bodily hygiene of the troop, rank and
file, recruits or seniors, soldiers re-enlisted: the bodies of
recruits for that so-called military service, obsessed
about the most physical functions; soldiers stricken by
infections and the basest urges in every bowel, knot,
ganglion, vessel, filter, muscle, artery and capillary; afire
with a forty-degree fever, childish, aggressive, always
ready to rub their hand, up and down, on their cock,
their cock out, its head red and clammy, manipulated,
rubbed up and down, moistened, wet with spit, with
soap, cream, wine, coffee, milk; with its shaft rubbed up
and down, manipulated, stained, coloured, greased with
cream, polished like black-and-yellow shoes, quinine,
tobacco, with cigarette, cigar or pipe ash.

'Always on and on, more and more often . . . until
the usual end, always the same, firm and stiff: the same

old mess-tin, mug; kept close by, at the start of the same old operation; ready, to fill, to the top, to overflowing with sperm-loads, shot, held back inside the foreskin, or ejaculated into a rag or handkerchief or wrapper or bag or beret or shoe or boot: fresh and luminous cum, blind, dumb, useless; spectre of worms and dimwits, holy dimwits, execrable matter to execrate, to scorn, to smear about until it is gone, hidden, diluted; to use with contempt, disdain, infection as submission, seizure and subjugation of different comrades-in-arms . . . from north or south, literate or illiterate, neat and tidy, meticulous: with the map of their underpants unsoiled, with no angry wives that shout from faraway, with no mugs and mess-tins that always smell of filth; who write and receive letters: letters to mother to father to grandfather to uncle to brother and sister and girlfriend, and also sometimes to the wife, to friends at the local cafe or workplace or cooperative society—these then get coated with cum, in pockets and plates, in wallets and in the envelopes of coveted letters. Buried in sperm, cancelled, infected, pushed away, cast down for ever, spurned, surpassed, surpassed by the very seed that smothers them, in the production, in the ostentatious and obsessive use of . . . in the taste for . . . in the hunger for . . . in the smell of . . . ; against boredom, order, memory, the bugle and . . .

'Those flies, companions of soldiers with afternoons and long confinements of distraction and maps:

in the end they always fly a strange route that leads them to land on the shiny tight tip of the erect cock that's being handled, manipulated; repetition, load, shoot, recoil; reload and re-handle; with a whirr of satisfaction, a chafing of wings, the blue and violet lamps lit beneath the wings, of bulbous lamps on the crown of the tip, and then a short march, with its feet, flicking its wings up now and then intermittently, then off again, quicker still, sure and easy directions, stopping, changing direction, trying a new passage in new directions in every sense, off again, testing out its wings, hurtling towards the prospect of a distant flight; then instead a dive bomb and chirring of the hairy nervature of its back, of its front legs, of its longer back legs, displaying and retracting its sting, turning its head 360 degrees around its invisible, inexistent neck . . .

'In the meantime the soldier watches spellbound . . . he has stopped his handling but has it firm in his grip, not knowing what thought to follow: no one knows why he is watching nor why he is handling . . . the round taste in his throat has lost its flavour . . . it can have no flavour in that place . . . there is no cloud, nor window, nor song; he watches without a thought, he avoids thinking . . . and to avoid thinking, he sees in the bed a brush that navigates like a hair-clad island . . . he gazes at the flies . . . but the mess-tin beside him is ready and waiting . . . gently exuding its filthy odour.

'So he looks for a glass . . . or a bottle or a cup that he can turn upside down on his cock to catch the fly; pull off its wings and so leave it alive to wander around the cot . . . to drop upside down onto the floor . . . by his boots . . . by the pictures of a whore giving a blowjob . . . ; the fly, having finished its sampling and some kind of attempt at digging, stops still; suddenly flies off, without even opening its wings, or opening its wings so fast that the soldier cannot see, almost with a leap, a jump like a flea . . . a missile.

'The soldier carries on and soon he fills the mess-tin . . . then sees that the fly is back . . . then hears the bugle and starts waiting for the return of the young recruits and malingerers to bury beneath his mountain of . . . And this is the greatest punishment the Italian Royal Army has constantly meted out to whole generations of soldiers . . . recruits from every part, from up and down the peninsula: a royal punishment for the whole of Italy for centuries and campaigns, barracks and battalions, camps and workshops, towns and cities, valleys, lanes, towers, caves, hovels, hamlets, houses, asylums, universities, seminaries, orphanages . . . '

TARQUINIO MARCACCI WAS ALSO TROUBLED by the thought that his son Traiano was alone at home in Fossombrone, of about the same age now as those Arab slaves who served the officers at their messes and also at their beds and couches, and therefore to some extent part and parcel of those deviant experiences he had seen and written about. To such an extent that on his return home to Fossombrone, once he had kissed and hugged his wife, his first act was to go and inspect his son's bed, and the underpants in his chest of drawers. Then, man to man, he asked also to see the pants he was wearing. There were no maps as such, though the impression of the first lands was already apparent in the cloth, those lands more easy to discover, discovered almost by chance, once there . . . in that place . . . in short, it became apparent that all zones had already been identified, their boundaries staked out, though not yet drawn. So he took his son immediately to the most dependable madam in the town, at Hotel . . .

Without too much explanation he showed him what to do by being the first to mount the large pink hulk of that indigenous two-humped camel. He soon dismounted to let his son climb on. He waited outside with fatherly discretion and to savour his paternal pride alone, smoking in the corridor, and when the newly initiated youth reappeared, he sent him off with a pat on the back and returned right away to the camel so that he could ruminate better, longer and more eagerly over the sweet and rediscovered taste of indigenous cinnamon.

TRAIANO WAS STANDING IN FRONT of his dead mother and trying to work out why and from where she stank so much of sulphur.

'From her knickers,' he concluded remembering his father's profitable instruction, to the point that he pronounced that irreverent word aloud.

He looked his mother in the face, along her nose, beyond her two yellow cheeks to her patch of moles and her ears. With his left hand he tried once again to close her eyelids: they were slender and dark as though they were no more than black dust; but instead they were damp and slimy like the layers of an onion . . . He chastised himself for that other spontaneous irreverence by bending down to free his mother of her shoes and handbag.

To keep his spirits up he said: 'Old hen . . . glorious old hen . . . pushy, squawking hen . . . You've finished squawking . . . squawking and begging . . . squawking and commanding . . . She hadn't wanted to give up her money. Hadn't wanted to sell the house . . . Less than two hours ago she had said no, then changed her mind, was persuaded to go and live in Rome . . . to meet and befriend the Duce's wife, Donna Rachele . . . Her signing of the document had killed her.'

He looked and saw her eyelids half open again, still haughty and suspicious. He wanted to try and view her with affection, at least with benevolence . . . but instead he could merely respect her. Yet he was amazed by his mother's fortitude: to die over a signature, so as not to leave her home . . . once again he railed against destiny . . . against the right-thinking bourgeoisie who have no idea how to die . . . not for their home, nor for their fatherland.

'The old sulphurous hen . . . instead of leaving her home she had preferred to die . . . right away . . . just like that . . . at the notary's desk . . . to notify her decision and intent straight away . . . a sulphurous fart, a large sulphurous turd . . . To ensure there was no doubt about where I'd have sent her . . . I certainly wasn't thinking of the Capuchin nuns . . . first to a hotel, for a month or so . . . for a start . . . then perhaps, from the hotel, she herself might have suggested going to live with the Capuchins, for some company . . . to spread sulphur in the countryside . . . the ambitious old hen.'

After his father's death she had begun spreading sulphur . . . more sugary and cloying... at first.

When his father died she had picked him up from beneath the table. She had wiped the soup from his chin and taken off his smoking jacket soaked in broth with scraps of boiled meat between the braids and tassels . . .

She had cleaned him and told him off . . . : 'Filthy beast . . . filthy swine . . . filthy hog, filthy pig, filthy animal . . . bull, bull for milk cows . . . swine, hog.'

MEANWHILE THE NEWS that Traiano Marcacci had carried his dead mother in his arms across the piazza and over the main street . . . in his arms, like an animal . . . had spread throughout the town causing disgust and admiration.

'How was he holding her? Hugging her, holding her against his cheek?' were the questions of those more naive and simple folk who tended towards respect.

'But was she actually dead? And not drooling from the mouth? Blood from the nose? When one says the peace of the dead, the laying out of the body, once the soul has departed . . . instead . . . like that . . . like a pauper, like some homeless wretch who had died of cold under a bridge. Ah . . . Marcacci, Marcacci,' remarked the bourgeoisie and everyone else who imitated them, who went on to add: 'What a stroke of luck for him, and for her too . . . who knows where he'd have sent her . . . He's suddenly free, nothing to stop him—he can go where he likes, with no regrets.'

At the funeral Marcacci walked tall and alone behind the hearse, greeting no one. He wore civilian dress, grey, though his black shirt could be seen under a blue scarf; and on his breast, half hidden by the lapels of his jacket, the gold medal his mother had been awarded two years earlier for services to education.

It was a second-class hearse, generally used for the lower ranks of society; for the poor who paid out of decency to avoid the frenzy and ignominy of a funeral done by the Congregation of Charity. It was the same priest who conducted those wretched processions, an eighty-year-old alcoholic who for many years had been known by everyone, including himself, as Tibis Quoque because of his slip-ups in Latin and all his alcoholic blunders.

Earlier that morning, in the cathedral, he had proceeded to finish off the host and empty the chalice in front of the women who were waiting for Communion. Having realized that none was left, he had displayed the empty chalice with its gilt interior and the solid silver tray, had turned in confusion to the altar, taken the ampulla of wine, returned in tears to the women, and made the gesture of offering them a sip of it, to drink.

On the hearse Marcacci had hung a long black drape interwoven with silver, fixed to one of the wrought-iron flames along the sides, and let it dangle over the coffin; every now and then he went and took hold of it, and continued like this for some distance.

The only mark of distinction he wanted was for the old elementary-school caretaker to follow one step behind carrying the tricolour banner of the Fossombrone Schools Association, the old and glorious symbol of advancement and progress: not exactly a Fascist banner but just as much a symbol of love for the fatherland and for its people.

OVER THE NEXT FEW DAYS, news spread that Marcacci had left by night for Rome, saying goodbye to no one.

The blue notepaper disappeared and Norma withdrew into a suffering that turned her pale, and her mouth clenched with a rigid blackness; and yet her hair shone more neatly and wavily than ever. She hid her grief and pallor from no one: in front of other people she clenched her mouth more tightly and let her arms and hands drop down, as if pleading for help. This was the behaviour Damìn liked; he stayed close to his mother as a gentle reminder that he understood and appreciated her suffering, the fervent expiation of her guilt. Likewise he stayed beside his grandfather to share with him that new understanding, that air of vigil that filled the house.

One evening, over supper, Damìn recounted aloud and in much detail the story of Traiano Marcacci's punishment and escape. He had found the strength and purpose of this story in his own victorious pride. The scandal could be avoided or at least tempered, instead of being heaped on the pain of his mother, whose conscience must have been so troubled as to need constant support.

Marcacci had demanded money from the owners of all the farms and other properties in Fossombrone. He said the money was for the Fascist authorities, who were protecting their lands and interests and all their activities. They had paid up for three years or so with no complaint, but the centurion had then become more greedy and rapacious, and more brazen. And here Damìn added something of his own: as if he had some personal experience in life, in his feelings and aspirations; some particular misfortune, loss or trouble, so that he could give vent to his personal feeling of revulsion. Marcacci had become so brazen, asking too much, almost the impossible, that some of the larger landowners had found the courage to go to Pesaro to report him. This then led to the arrival of the provincial secretary, the confrontation, accusation and expulsion from the party. And then the escape of the proud Marcacci, who could not endure such great humiliation before the whole town. He had attempted to defend himself in front of the provincial secretary, and afterwards, at the club and in the piazza, accusing everyone of ingratitude, especially the usual bourgeoisie, he had complained out loud to all the members of his squad about how the Fascist Party was kowtowing to the Church, that it was repudiating the first and most important principles of the revolution and the March on Rome, and that its officials were now conniving with the Freemasons and the Jews to appease the old powers and good-for-nothings. And that he was off to Rome, not to escape or hide but to unmask all these shenanigans and betrayals by the bourgeoisie and the new bourgeoisie of renegades.

Damìn's words became more enthusiastic when he saw how his story had touched his mother, but also because his feeling of revulsion for her and the lover who had betrayed her was turning into admiration— above all for Marcacci's brazenness, for his bullying and thuggery, for causing pain and exploiting others. These others, the landowners, had brought his comeuppance, and this could be an example, however painful, for his mother, who had withdrawn into her own suffering, turning pale and trembling with weakness. In the plot by the landowners and the action of the provincial secretary he could taste his own revenge. His story kept his mother in suspense, like the flame of a kiln that never lowers during the firing, but gradually increases and spreads, licking the pots below, those smaller and more delicate, so that the kiln's closed walls heat everything thoroughly until it reaches that peak of red heat in the firing. From that moment you had to wait until the walls cooled and gradually lost their colour; and when it was cool enough to hold a hand over it, and was a pale orange, then it was time to open up, to uncover and remove the finished work. At the end of his whole story Damìn rested his right palm on his mother's arm.

THAT EVENING IN BED his pride and his suffering were both at one: outside was the picture of Marcacci wandering around Rome, running away in protest, in a Rome of ancient ruins, ditches and catacombs. Outside also, the twin picture of Occhialini in prison, he too somewhere near Rome, covered in blood and half-naked, incarcerated in an empty cell, his hands incapable of work, with no tools, unable to speak and with his filthy head slumped onto his even filthier chest.

Next day a rumour went round that Marcacci had gone to Rome not just because of his expulsion from the Fascist Party and his humiliation but also to get treatment for a bad dose of venereal disease. Fortunately for Damìn, it was also said that the centurion had contracted this bad dose in Rome itself, back in the days of the glorious march. And now, almost fourteen years later, it had reappeared.

XIII

1936. The Empire and Its Treasures.
Tarzan's Girlfriend. The Ice-Cream Girl

His exact awareness, concerning his own body and the whole sphere of his unhappiness, of the passing of time and the arrival of a new year, 1936, as well as his own home, was made clear to him by an item of little importance, reported in his grandfather's newspaper, at the bottom of a page. During 1936, experiments with television in America had made great progress, with possibilities, if not actual practical results, in their application for industry.

In four days it would be New Year. Only far-off events and dates, particularly of a scientific, almost fantastical kind, could disturb Damìn's time, abstract and whole, drawing him away from that vase of his, always brimming with sorrow, moving him and cleaving him with different ideas and preoccupations.

Not even the war in Africa could give him an exact sense of time passing; nor did he notice any importance in the relationship between his own age and that of the soldiers he so admired for their weapons, their battles and the explorations they could make, and for the colonial helmet they wore on their heads. The battles and victories were taking place, not far away on some distant African territory, but in his inner film, affecting almost his state of mind, driving or distracting him from the confused meanderings of his pain. He followed the war on a map nailed to the beam in his bedroom, and there, behind the colours and the words, he looked about for a figure to clothe: a legionary, an officer, a gold prospector or a coffee planter, among those heaps of treasures and pointers on the map that signified mines, natural resources, fields, crops in the beautiful land of Abyssinia.

He also looked for Marcacci who had gone straight there, among the first, at the head of an intrepid legion, the bravest, in constant skirmishes with the enemy, bloodthirsty hordes armed with arrows and poisoned spears.

Marcacci's absence had increased the emptiness of Fossombrone as well as the surroundings of his own life: each object in it seemed inert, each disjointed from the other. Even his grandfather moved silently over the joint backdrop of pain that constituted time present, isolated and monotonous, and which conserved the colour and aroma of Occhialini's lacquer.

Yet his mother remained conspicuously absent, in some mobile point, so that she could be shifted about and not seen, put elsewhere, pulled inside or propelled up. Vitina kept abreast of the time, silent and submissive like a good vase, a small cheap cooking pot, useful for company and for silence, or for taking fresh food to the cinema.

At the cinema they sat in one of the first three rows of cold, cast-iron seats: hand in hand, they abandoned themselves to the world, to adventure, both floating into those unknown realities; together they roamed each scene and setting in the jungle or on the ocean, or in large foreign cities. It was more difficult for them, at least in Damìn's mind, to share those scenes set in Italian cities they knew by name alone, or in musicals, or all those stories where the actors were constantly singing: tenors and arias, pianists or open-mouthed women, all tra-la-las and ringlets. It was impossible for them to enter the bedrooms or drawing rooms of rich people in evening dress. Damìn couldn't bear their stupid love stories with happy endings—their interminable kissing on the mouth, eyes closed, with soft quivering eyebrows, with great close-ups of their faces right across the screen.

Best of all he enjoyed costume films, with war and arm-to-arm combat; then films involving African exploration and conquest, and then American cowboy and gangster films. Gangsters were the only men he could watch falling in love, hugging and kissing a woman, without him feeling uncomfortable. Their women were usually blond and tomboyish and had much of the fallen woman about them; and they knew how to deal with a slap in the face and could fend off more serious threats, often with a smile and a wink: two large gleaming and understanding eyes, even when in pain and brimming with tears. The actresses in love stories or musical comedies were unbearable, to be avoided, not even to be looked at, in their long white gowns, tied with buttons and laces, with the flat pearly necklines, dressed up to look invincible. The dancers in these films were also fake, acting with mechanical gestures: their bare porcelain legs immobile, even when moving around at the speed of a tap dance, looking like those in billboard posters, at the top of which they wore shorts made not of cloth but of some light, flimsy material, which ended at the ankles with shoes just as fake, brightly coloured, that looked as though they could be neither unlaced nor taken off.

The only undressed woman he could bear was Jane, Tarzan's girlfriend. The only actress for whom he had any feeling of love was Virginia Bruce, a sassy blonde who wore lamé and sequin dresses, the indomitable companion of a gangster, Public Enemy Number One, who had her face reshaped by a plastic surgeon so as not to be recognized.

MEANWHILE MASTURBATION PROCEEDED on a daily basis, repeated sometimes twice or thrice a day, now with a fixed repertory of images and fantasies, sometimes added to by new figures. Masturbating, more than bringing satisfaction, was the affirmation of those ideas in his head and in his mind that were finally reconciled and united with his whole body, in a whole dimension of its own, though free and roaming, mutable. Indeed, in both the choice of images and its ritual and practice to the point of pleasure, it became the measure of his own capacity to think, to act, to possess a knowledge that was entirely subject to its own will and its own capacities. And in the end, apart from satisfaction, he could consider himself more mature, even in his guilt, before his own pain.

News arrived from Abyssinia that Marcacci had been wounded in arm-to-arm combat against the troops of Ras Seyoum and decorated with a silver medal on the field.

To follow the events of the war, the Possanza family had bought a radio that regularly broadcast musical entertainments and many songs that Vitina in particular enjoyed listening to. Brother and sister would dance together; it was she who would start by lifting her right arm: tangos and slow waltzes were their favourites.

Those dances let Damìn get closer to his sister, after almost everything had been taken away with his mother's decision to give them separate bedrooms and that he would sleep in the room above. Vitina had formed two small breasts that were firm when he nudged them with his elbow. Her ringlets took much brushing each day, dropped down to her waist, and were always tied with a ribbon. She was clever at school, and at home every now and then, during long periods of reading and writing at the dining table, she would pull out a secret exercise book and write lines and whole poems.

At the cinema she too preferred adventure films, especially those with pirates, but at home she read stories not so much about love, written for little girls, as those recounting long family sagas. She spent whole weeks stuck into reading *The Rains Came* and *Gone with the Wind*, refusing even to go with her brother to the cinema.

Damìn read little, and no longer even bought *L'Avventuroso*; from time to time he took out his *Mickey Mouse* album and *Tim Tyler's Luck*. But he enjoyed reading *Martin Eden* and *White Fang*; he loved the exploits of Don Quixote, and enjoyed even more the adventures of a little boy he immediately thought of as a brother, Lazarillo de Tormes, who was far more fortunate than he in having neither family nor home, and could spend his whole time travelling the world, far away from Fossombrone.

Meanwhile the war continued triumphantly, with frequent processions and events in the town to which everyone gladly went; even those from the villages, even the farm workers from the surrounding areas. Everyone was delighted by the victories and the conquests because everyone expected to get rich in Africa, to leave their jobs, emigrate and colonize magnificent lands that were easy to farm and laden with fruit trees.

Even his grandfather went to the piazza on the day the empire was proclaimed, but not with a black shirt, and only after the Duce had finished his speech: he had preferred to listen to it on the radio at home, through the door from the next room. His daughter-in-law had also listened to the speech, standing at the window looking out at the garden. They were alone at home, silent, before and after the radio. Possanza had eventually gone out, embarrassed by that silence, and to stop himself wondering whether she, still gazing at the sky outside the window, was waiting for the return of Marcacci, now more glorious than before.

Damìn and Lavinia were placed in separate rows at school but continued to keep an eye on each other.

Now at the cinema there were documentaries on the war in Africa, the speeches of the Duce, and the many Fascist rallies in cities throughout Italy.

Italian soldiers were shown advancing confidently and cautiously, well armed with guns, bayonets and cartridge belts, accompanied by machine-guns, light artillery, lorries loaded with other weapons, ammunition and supplies. Bersaglieri on bicycles and motor bikes went to occupy a fortress, lowered the enemy flag and instantly hoisted the tricolour. It fluttered in the African wind, bright and rectangular, while the enemy flags hung limply as though sodden. The enemy was held captive, in disorderly array, with arms raised and hands crossed above their heads, wounded and submissive. Their weapons were piled on the ground: swords in the sand, guns too long, belts abandoned and piled together, never to be worn again.

The new land of the empire could be seen with wide horizons and mountains, unknown trees, massive or small. Hills with many folds, just like soft clay. The forests were rugged but tall, and could be driven through easily in a car, or even better in a truck with caterpillar tracks. The villages could be seen, invariably low beneath a hill, with huts of mud and straw, open at the top, round, and built one next to the other in a circle. Dogs wandered furtively with distended stomachs and their tails between their legs, but with huge, sly, menacing eyes. The eyes of the black unarmed villagers or prisoners were also wide open and white, but their gaze was fixed and kindly. And yet the eyes of the people and the dogs seemed to resemble one another and to be searching one another out, and they soon assembled in a line that took up the whole landscape.

The Duce stood at the balcony, majestic yet lively, with restless movements repeated almost in jest. Damìn remembered those words: 'puppet of the bourgeoisie', and soon rediscovered his own pain amid that gaiety and noise. But Italy now had an empire; and he in turn, before too long, could go there to work, to set up his own pottery, new and different, yet following his grandfather's principles.

THAT SUMMER, HAVING IMMEDIATELY PASSED the June exams, he worked hard with his grandfather at the pottery. He made a series of cooking pots in the traditional shapes and sizes, which he then decorated in his own style, with a blue-green sprig. His grandfather smiled and encouraged him while his father disapproved. He also learnt to load the kiln and then to fill it with bundles of sticks and split logs that would burn at different rates during the firing. He himself made the wall that closed the kiln but wanted his grandfather to light it.

He found satisfaction in these tasks and during that summer he could feel some sign of growing up.

At the end of August he fell in love with the girl who sold ice cream at the main cafe. She had black plaits and a fresh face into which the whiteness of her features merged; but her eyes were so large that they disappeared around either side of her face: so that her eyelashes were always quivering and two thin blue lines ran across her temple. He stopped to watch her as she carefully filled each ice-cream cone, choosing one by one the scoops for each flavour. He went often to buy an ice cream, asking always just for chocolate so that the girl wouldn't have to take too long looking down to choose. He also wanted to be remembered for the monotony of his request, which ought then to indicate the paucity of his expectations that reduced him inevitably to inextinguishable misery with little desire to live.

He spent hours and hours each day watching the girl, from nine in the morning till supper time. She finished work, went out into the piazza and almost ran to get home, crossing the main street to the via Flaminia, then through the square, down by the hospital to the vegetable plots behind, and up towards the Capuchin monastery. She lived in a small isolated house that stood sidelong at the top of a market garden. Her father and mother were market gardeners: she had gone to college. She had no brothers or sisters, nor any friends, or at least none with whom she was ever seen. She had a beautiful name, Cecilia, and her surname was not one of those that belonged to Fossombrone, at least so far as Damìn knew. Her father must have been a farm worker, one of those who hadn't been able to keep a farm due to some illness or because they had a young family.

One Sunday in September, when it was now cooler and hardly anyone was going to buy ice cream, Damìn managed to get up closer to the ice-cream girl's face and body on the pretext of looking inside the ice-cream trough; he could feel her breath and could see her gums between her open lips—thick and grainy, pink between droplets of saliva. It revolted him, like a sickness, like a disease. That revulsion remained with him for a long time—it mixed indissolubly with his own saliva even at a distance, in his more tender memories of her; yet he continued to hear the ring of her voice as she served, politely and intelligently, like the ring of a beautiful earthenware jug.

And so something of Cecilia remained with him: a true quality that would belong with him for ever, as genuine as that hint of understanding and hope shared by two solitary people. He spent the whole of September making jars and dishes from morning to evening, hoping to give that sweet and unmistakable touch to his pottery. He signed the larger vases and dishes with a D.P. like his grandfather but used a stronger blue and wrote them in separate block capitals in modern style.

And thus he passed his time as a potter, and his youth, forming his letters in rigid strokes, each distinct from the other. Little happened, but those things that did were very great and cloaked by mystery—the same mystery that filled every pot at the moment it was moulded, fired and sent out into the world. Forever filled with that breath of his that would never be poured out.

XIV

The Conqueror. The Sword of the Ras. Bosambo

MARCACCI ARRIVED IN FOSSOMBRONE on the third
Sunday of October. He appeared in the piazza at eleven,
at the end of Mass, dressed as a military consul, wearing
a colonial pith helmet, with his wife, tall and skinny as
a rake, grey, the daughter of an army general from
Piemonte who was a friend of Marshall Badoglio.

Marcacci gazed at everyone proudly and held his
wife like a weapon, as he basked in self-glory with rib-
bons on his breast and the medal, the great silver medal,
that hung down covering part of his heart. On his belt
he no longer wore his mother-of-pearl dagger but a
kind of short sabre, of a colour between old gold and
bronze, of exotic appearance, dented and engraved with
an infinity of lines, curving down to a thin shiny point.
The weapon appeared to be covered with writing, fash-
ioned with labour and determination, tinged with
hatred, unsheathed, naked, fresh from shedding blood.
It was an ancient Coptic dagger that he himself had
seized from the hands of Ras Sejoum during the arm-
to-arm combat in which he and his intrepid comrades
had thrashed the Negus' finest army, wounded and

captured his favourite cousin, stormed a strategic position decisive for the whole war, and earned on the field the silver medal for military valour. It was said that without those crimes of extortion and villainy that had sent him away from Fossombrone, from that pit of envy and malice, the medal would certainly have been gold. But all the same, the silver glinted and dazzled the whole piazza where all its citizens had gathered to share the solemn hour of noon on that fine Sunday of October.

Marcacci studied each individual and group, and when he acknowledged a greeting he did so with measured sternness. He remained alone, next to his noble military wife, shunning invitations and company. He was there just to be seen and to gaze at the others who had to gaze at him. Damìn also gazed at him, from a distance, from behind a group of farmers, rocked by the desire to approach him, to reread on his mouth the voice of authority, to catch the moist warmth of his lips, to recognized the curls around his neck and ears. Marcacci didn't once take off his pith helmet, nor did he ever lower or turn his head; nor did he even snort with an air of irritation and menace as he used to do constantly in the piazza before he went away. Damìn studied the new dagger: he admired it and feared it, and it seemed odd in place of the other—that other dagger had been murderous too but associated, intimately, with his own gashes and wounds. Which he could in some way compare with a large billhook of the kind used by a village peasant, a wild cutthroat, a ruthless overseer. But this figure, though familiar and more approachable for Damìn, seemed very vague and didn't match the picture he had of Marcacci: his dagger-billhook remained alien, detached and distant from all the images of the new relationship Damìn had hoped to rebuild with that honoured soldier who had been both his enemy and his leader. He remained an enemy, bristling, aloof, through an African magic.

Marcacci remained there in the piazza until two o'clock, thus delaying the whole town's Sunday lunch, making them almost ignore the particular dishes of that day through their discussions and wonderment, their enthusiasms and recollections, warnings and predictions in which all the people of Fossombrone became involved, partly through pride, partly fear. What would a figure of such great authority now become in Fossombrone and in the whole province? Provincial secretary, prefect, chief magistrate perhaps, of Pesaro or Ancona? And with a rich aristocratic wife, connections in the army, and even with the royal family.

BY THE AFTERNOON, contrary to the general custom at that time of autumn for the townsfolk to close themselves up in a club, cafe, tavern, they were back in the piazza on the hunt for news and forecasts, all of them, apart from two leading lawyers, one linked to the

Church, the other to certain landowners, and the local vet with antifascist leanings who had been called to a providential swine epidemic in Fratterosa. Possanza the potter certainly wasn't there; his anarchic and artistic sensibilities led him to prefer his own company. But his son Dorino was there, a Fascist neither of rank nor distinction, a trader eager though unreliable, sometimes there sometimes not, and only when it fitted in with his timetable and commitments as a travelling salesman with his awnings, pots, banks and bills of credit. Many, on seeing him, might have started thinking about his wife, the beautiful Norma who had once, it was said, been one of Marcacci's secret lovers—a passing, predatory fling, one of those women that are just a number and a name but who don't last long for a womanizer like him. Dorino couldn't even understand why all those people were there, as he made his way to the cafe that awaited him, the second in order of prestige.

Before going to the cinema, Damìn went back to the piazza with his sister just to see Marcacci again and to point him out to her. He was prepared even to miss the first show, the best, full of whole new surprises, the most action-packed and entertaining for all the youngsters of the town, the 2.15 show, briefly preceded by the Luce newsreel.

Damìn crossed the crowded piazza but couldn't see the commandant; he was disappointed and thought of his mother. She had kept silent through lunch, head bent, watching the other plates as though worried she might miss the appropriate moment to refill or change them. She must have heard news of Marcacci's return in church, or must have seen him unexpectedly, standing there erect in the centre of the square, veteran cloaked in glory, with his wife at his side, as though keeping guard.

Damìn found his mother's silence painful and, at the end of lunch, asked curtly whether she was going off for a walk, or to church, to make her understand he had discovered her secret and was pursuing her pitilessly in her guilt and bewilderment.

MARCACCI SUDDENLY APPEARED at the edge of the piazza, alone, without his colonial helmet. He was all the more handsome since he no longer belonged to any of them, or to Fossombrone, disowned and therefore lost for good. Not even Damìn, javelin thrower, junior team, regional champion under his command, could go up and greet him. He too had to be content to admire him from a distance, noting what changes had been brought about by the great exploits of one of the empire's most valiant soldiers. How much more must Marcacci's beauty and power have weighed on his mother's sorrowful mind: his image radiant above the immense void of his absence. Who knows what might have been said, or was said, by those simpering and sanctimonious old women, the only people from whom she could obtain information: how they would have seen, and with what vague and inappropriate illusions and words they would describe his beauty and gravity, the magnificence of his figure and the slow manner of his gestures. What could they have said about that dagger, which not even Damìn could look upon?

And so, to get things clear for his mother's sake as well as for the whole story of his own pain, Damìn continued watching Marcacci while he and Vitina wandered up and down along the edge of the piazza. Meanwhile Marcacci's wife had returned and stood once again like a pole beside her husband. Vitina gazed at the woman and said she looked nasty as well as ugly. Damìn was glad about his sister's remark, and for a moment he felt as if both he and his mother had been avenged. Glad also that his mother's beauty had been acknowledged and confirmed, though indirectly, as being superior and insuperable. In that instant he remembered that she, at home, beautiful and sorrowful at a window or at a mirror, had the company of his grandfather—the two of them alone if not together, close to each other in the rooms of the house and through its doorways, touched in the same way by the sounds from the garden and those still louder sounds from the rushing waters of the river.

HE WATCHED THE FILM, not feeling fully absorbed: perhaps for the first time in his life at a film of that kind.
The song of the black chief seemed more about his and
his mother's sorrow than about slavery and the jungle:
his sorrows merged with those strange deep notes of
the black man and joined and rose up in a single note,
until they were lost in the drumbeats. The film also had
a river—broad, meandering in among the breadfruit
trees, but then violent and intersected by numerous
waterfalls that marked the end of the tribe's territory.
His own fluvial territory had always been the sandy
bend of the Metauro after the first bridge of
Fossombrone, where the wheelbarrows and carts of the
diggers and quarrymen went down, all people who,
according to his grandfather, had no love for the river,
who damaged it with their excavating, destroying its
banks and currents . . . so that one day the bridges
would collapse, and even the walls . . . and the whole
town into the sand.

As soon as the film was over Damìn went home to
find his mother. His grandfather was still in his room,
though he should have been at the cafe, Fossombrone's
largest, more than an hour ago. His mother was standing,
as he had imagined, at the French window gazing at
the garden.

'I've seen Marcacci,' said Damìn impulsively, 'my
old centurion friend. He's back from Africa. Wearing a

big colonial hat and a prince's dagger. Not looking at anyone, not even turning his head. He has a wife beside him, taller than him, skinny, daughter of a general.'

But at his first words his mother had gone off to her room. Damìn moved across the dining room in the opposite direction. He was now at the window, with his forehead on the glass, and began to sing Bosambo's song. He carried on like this, following a film that was completely different to the one he had seen, continually altering the theme, forcing the notes lower than his voice. He was surprised then by Lavinia who was angry he had disappeared when they came out of the cinema, and that he hadn't liked the film, which was actually really lovely.

Damìn tried to remember the film but stopped once more at the black man's face and the song. He hadn't managed to give it his usual attention since, each time Bosambo smiled and sang, he exposed two thick gums that resembled those of Cecilia, the ice-cream girl.

XV

Marseille. The Mother's Letter. The Turtle Dove.
Kisses. Fear

ON 4 NOVEMBER, NATIONAL HOLIDAY and day of celebration, Damìn received a postcard just as he was leaving
for the parade. It was from Occhialini, from Marseille.
The stamp and postmark were French, clear and
readable. The picture showed a large port full of ships,
with signs, shop windows, and the tables of a cafe
behind to the right, on the quay. On the other side
was written: 'A cordial (and not very imperial) souvenir
from Marseille with greetings and many good wishes
from Amilcare Occhialini, cobbler.' The postmark bore
the date 28 October,* chosen deliberately as part of the
message.

That evening, Damìn discovered from the ency-
clopedia that Marseille was a large Mediterranean port,
a Roman city, expanded in more recent times by Italian
engineering and labour—a popular seaport and commercial centre for Africa and the Middle East, known
for its illegal trade in weapons drugs and sex, associated

* Anniversary of Mussolini's March on Rome in 1922.

with criminals of every kind, port of embarkation for the foreign legion and penal colonies of Martinique and the Caribbean, controlled by violent gangs in constant feud, haven for slave traders, subversives and outlaws, with bands of gypsies and bandits camped by nearby lagoons and canebrakes to the south and south-west.

Occhialini had therefore chosen the right city, where evil could be practised daily, and daily the lives of other people could be attacked with words, as with a cobbler's skiving knife.

Damìn's grandfather saw the postcard and remarked amiably: 'Occhialini, Amilcare . . . there's a good man, courageous and honest . . . intelligent too, always working for liberty. In France . . . he's ended up in France—that's good. I'm glad he's writing to you, remembers you, sends his greetings. It's a shame you can't reply, he certainly won't have given his address. But keep this postcard . . . as a reminder, a souvenir. You never know—you might find some time or other . . . '

Damìn didn't take kindly to these last words from the person he loved most in all the world: the prophecy contained in them sounded even worse than the unjust, ingenuous clemency of his comments—worse perhaps than Occhialini's postcard itself. What was he actually supposed to do to become an adult? What was he then supposed to do when he had done so, alone and far from Fossombrone? Anything other than imitating and going looking for Occhialini. He would have to move alone, following his own devices; he would always be poised on the black spout of that vase of his, drawing up time and breath, hard together, both made of clay, to purify and to separate.

Even the poets he read at school offered him no solutions; nor did they expect him to go alone. Even the Fascist Party seemed to organize and order him to all their parades to make sure he was not alone. But Fascism was also for those who were more wily and clueless, for the hypocrites, for liars, big talkers always smiling and alert and always anxious to please. Nor did he have his eyes on America, the great prairies, Jack London's continent of ice. *L'Avventuroso* was just what it was . . . a comic, an illusion. Could he really ever imagine meeting Queen Luana? He who couldn't even chat up the ice-cream girl or stop her in the street? Not even the palest and poorest of girls in Fossombrone, daughter of the man who digs vegetables for the friars. Yet he would have to leave his mother, the most beautiful and unhappy, most guilty and most whorish woman in the world. Not even at the cinema did a son have to endure so much, and go as far as he had gone, so infinitely far away . . . yet always reaching the brim of his own jug, cold or red-hot depending on the laws of the rest of the world, all affecting his whole blood . . . too whole, too, too in everything.

And even to leave Lavinia, Vitina, the most tender, pale, innocent and defenceless of sisters. Vitina already had thighs and curly hairs on her groin and under her armpits; but she was still as white and smooth as a turtle dove over the river when it swoops down with wings closed, or a plaster dove on the fireplace that turns more dusty and gold each day . . . and mustn't be touched, for fear it might get smashed, into a thousand pieces . . . for fear of leaving finger marks in the dust, over its colour.

Marseille certainly wasn't a city for breeding turtle doves, nor for potters. Rome would certainly be more fitting, full of ancient monuments and holes dug into the tufa. But Rome too seemed only half-habitable, full of Fascists and aristocrats and echoing with the impossible roar of the Duce's speeches. It would have been difficult to cross the great asphalt piazza where every consular road converges from all directions in the world.

A little later, in bed, at the top of the staircase, in the small attic room, narrow but open to all the drafts across the beams and the endless sound of knocking, he found himself thinking he would be gone from Fossombrone before he had to leave for military service —with a school diploma, towards northern Europe, Holland, Norway. Or to Greece, to excavate monuments, or explore old cities, *o acontistés*, great thrower of darts and glances, still more subtle and faster than the faithful javelin, '*o acontistés*, sad youth who contents himself . . . '

And so his thoughts wandered off in search of images for his evening masturbation: he looked for images of Dutch and Norwegian girls but then was taken by the sight of the black sex of women at the port of Marseille, the open-armed protagonists of that sumptuous underworld. Then he went back to the usual images of his discoveries, childish joys, glimpsed, caught from behind doors and fences, in the streets, along the river, in the countryside among the corn.

He repeated the operation in the morning, trying again with Marseille and its port, with French and oriental women, their pleasure at making love with Italians; but once again he turned back to himself, to that usual space, for the experience that could all be concentrated in a fruit the size of an orange, with its bright peal split, torn, dripping. Meanwhile he caught the voice of the river displaying the mood of the new day: the amorous propensity of each thing, from wild plants to vegetable plots, caper flowers in the walls, the windows, the casements of the houses, cooking stoves, women undressed, his mother's bathrobe, when it was still untainted, untouched by Marcacci's contagion: the morning, amorous on slices of bread, on the milk jug; he became almost lost in regret. Then he moved forward, went all of a sudden to Cerignola, the girl in his class, to the mother of his friend who used to watch her through the keyhole, to the gym mistress, a temporary teacher, surprised by a whole class while making love with a boy from the top class in the gym on the mattress used for Greco-Roman wrestling, or the two sisters at the station who ran off with some soldiers in transit, not even would-be officers or petty officers, but simple, southern, dark-skinned soldiers on the baggage train.

Having paid the price, the day became just like every other day, with some small difference around the brim of the jug ... a film, an errand, a book, more time than usual with Vitina, the company of his mother, the pitiful spectacle of all his anxieties and all his bare deceits in the net of his guilt.

The day could be spent according to the fixed routines of obligations and duties, marked by alternating moments of pain and endurance. Fortunately in the winter there was more dancing with Vitina and fun and games, followed by plenty of pretend fighting on the edge of the bed or the ottoman.

SHORTLY BEFORE CARNIVAL, their mother, seized by a sudden impatience while she was sewing a costume for Lavinia, went off and called Damìn to her bedroom. She sat dishevelled at the mirror, unbuttoned, with her bra out like a whore ... and with an enormous round thigh protruding like an earthenware jar, and of the same pale colour—looking like one of those women who sold themselves to soldiers, of the kind who once, it is said, lived in the arches along the walls of the river, towards the cemetery, or like those other women in country villages who kept taverns or who tanned leather, with two or three rough or thieving husbands or lovers, witches or bone healers, all ready to sell themselves to the first man, pilgrim, platoon or army that went past; with soldiers lined up at the door, one after the other: able to service fifty in succession, or eighty or a hundred, provided they could plant their bums on something hard, outside the broken bed-springs, on the floor or even on stone.

But his mother had not an ounce of courage despite her appearance, not a single trace of shameless-ness in that whole tangle of her body, hair, breast, mouth and foot. And she couldn't just have rested her bum on something hard to transform herself . . . An unhappy beauty, pale and implacable as a ray of sun at dawn, gripped her and unravelled her like a skein of cotton.

'Come,' she said, 'take this letter to Signora Giampaoli, manageress at the social club. Tell her it's from me . . . and tell her kindly to deliver it by whatever means, even in person, just so long as it's safe . . . she knows who it's for. If she doesn't recognize you, tell her it's a letter from your mother, Norma Possanza, Norma Coramboni that was, Coramboni from Urbino, and tell her it's very important, yes, urgent.'

She paused and then, still holding the letter, added, with a tone less desperate: 'It's a letter about something to do with me . . . it's personal. Damìn, try to understand.'

Damìn took the letter straight to the manageress and despite his nervousness, touched by his mother's insistence and dejection, he tried to catch a glimpse of those rooms where the most prominent figures of Fossombrone and the nearby towns could be seen. The club had a narrow passageway that opened onto a room dense with smoke, oppressive also for its lighting and its velvets. It was a place inaccessible, generally regarded as a secret front, peripheral to the town but influential in all and everything to do with the town itself and all its citizens. Signora Giampaoli was not in the least surprised, either by the message or the boy's nervousness, and put the letter straight into the drawer of a table outside the dressing room and cloakroom. Damìn saw that on the same table there was even a telephone.

'Tell your mother I'll do my best to deliver the letter. I don't know when, but I'm quite sure I'll manage it. Though I cannot guarantee an answer.'

She looked as if she wanted to say something else to him, but changed her mind and sent him off with a

brisk smile, over some opinion or thought she didn't
want to express.

CARNIVAL WAS ALWAYS FOLLOWED by a period of
gloom, occupied by school duties as well as deadlines
and financial commitments for his grandfather, which
troubled them to the point of hampering his work. The
round of visits to banks and the offices of notaries and
lawyers was the most thankless task imaginable, but
one the master craftsman could not avoid, through duty
as well as lack of confidence in his son's ability to
administrate.

Dorino was always full of plans, complications, sudden whims, and careless too. He knew only how to sell
or, rather, purport to sell, with so much bluster that in
the end even the most enthusiastic buyers grew tired
and went off, with a cracked jar and not enough pots.
And he talked to everyone about aluminium—about
the advantages, practicality, hygiene of aluminium.

Added to the usual round of invoices and credit
notes were heavy bureaucratic demands imposed by the
new Fascist institutions on craft workers, commerce,
employment, sickness and industrial accidents, as well
as public holidays and fairs—even rules about the
amount of light and space in workshops, as well as the
periodical declaration of stock, production figures, sales,
turnover.

What happens when an old farmer's wife is billed for a jar or a cooking pot and she pays half in cash and half in geraniums or basil plants? Or when in fact she buys on credit with the promise of two dozen eggs at Easter and a pair of pigeons by mid-August, and you already know she'll find it hard to get through the winter and doesn't even have a chicken house or a pigeon loft?

The markets were ever poorer, and all goods getting more expensive, due also to the economic sanctions imposed on Italy by the League of Nations.

Nothing was arriving from the empire: no wealth and no new jobs. Some men, mostly labourers from smaller villages, just to get away for something to do, not to burden their families and their own consciences as hapless and hopeless fathers, had joined up as volunteers in another war, in Spain—a war between Spaniards, remote and ruthless, but well paid.

IN THE POSSANZA HOUSE the friction between the master craftsman and his son increased, over every problem and truth: over the situation and management of the pottery as well as the choice of products and markets. Dorino wanted to mortgage everything, to buy a big truck and trailer, apply for another licence and set up a much bigger business selling crockery and domestic equipment, including aluminium, enamel, iron, glass, steel, rubber. 'Everything for the modern home' was his motto.

Damiano put his faith in the pottery and in his work, sure about the beauty and utility of his vases and pots and their material and historical superiority over every other article of their kind. Damìn supported his grandfather, ever more convinced and attached to tradition through his own enthusiasm and passion, and much more critical than his grandfather about Dorino's animosity. But Dorino mortgaged the house and garden, added other debts and bought the latest new Fiat diesel truck with a Bartoletti trailer: both of them built for use as circus wagons, with 'Damiano & Dorino Possanza—Fossombrone' in red over the doors of the cab and 'Everything for the home' in still larger letters.

'Everything apart from common sense,' Damiano Possanza had muttered, while others in the town had added their own particular slogans, always with a touch of malice, such as: 'Everything including cuckold horns . . . to hang behind the door.'

But Dorino was quite oblivious and went off proudly on his first journey to a fair he'd never been to before, in Forlì. He came back two days later, having sold well, though much had been broken inside the wagons on the journey because of the way he had hurriedly loaded and unloaded the goods. But he felt sure he could establish a commercial network from Rimini to Senigallia, along the coast, and higher up, from Pergola to Urbino. Later they could go as far as Arezzo, Città di Castello, Gubbio, up the Adriatic coast to Forlì, and down to Ancona. He was already thinking about a second truck for his son, who would soon be grown up. Alone, back home in the evening, tired from his fairs and half-drunk, he was already pondering how to build links with the province's more successful industrialists, in bricks and timber, carbon coke and iron, how to approach the Solazzi of Fano, or Mancini and Dolci of Pesaro.

'Ancona? Forlì? My jugs have gone as far as Paris ... well transported and well esteemed,' said Damiano. 'Aluminium will soon be everywhere in the markets as well as the shops, while our vases and pots, we alone can make and sell these.' But throughout the summer period his son Dorino remained with the truck down at the coast, going here and there to fairs and markets, following also the new fashions of the holidaymakers.

DAMÌN WAS HAPPIER AT HOME without his father, whose absences had been frequent over the past few years; but now he could measure time in whole weeks and months, during which he could work out his own plans and ideas.

His mother remained alone in the house each afternoon, until the evening when the other three came back from the pottery. Vitina also went to be with her grandfather, if only to sit reading and writing among the clay and the bowls. One afternoon she began ordering and numbering by type, shape and series the various decorations used by the Possanzas, including her brother's latest sprig motifs. Then she wrote a sort of catalogue, with a page for each kind of pot, on which she drew and coloured the relevant decoration. She chose the oldest design, a leaf used in 1731 on five-litre jugs for taverns, used it as the coat of arms of the Possanza family, and decided to embroider it in brown and turquoise green onto a cloth for the dining table. Damìn feared it would mean the end of the old velveteen cloth of the desert and the oasis, which had truly been among his most valued companions in life— unkind, cruel, but indispensable. Damìn was working busily on a new thought that brought comfort: to continue his education he had to leave Fossombrone and move to Urbino or Fano, or take the train back and forth from five in the morning to five in the evening with his old friend Jenner. One of the workers, an older woman of around forty employed as a kneader, had also invited him to her house.

Two days after her first invitation she had candidly repeated that she would gladly welcome a fine youth like him, well mannered and strong; her husband was now bored and often away, and she still had the desire and the body of a young girl, as well as the fancy and experience of a free woman, 'almost of a woman of the city'. This final comment struck Damìn as some kind of reference to his mother. The woman, called Lena, was still quite attractive, even charming in her uncompromising workaday fashion. In the evening she went to wash herself under the spout of the main pump and exposed her golden neck beneath her tangle of black curls, and her more tender thighs above her sun- and earth-baked knees. Years earlier she had had a son, but he had died as a child in her arms, in a fit of convulsions.

'Misery,' she'd proclaim, 'Hell and misery,' she would often repeat with a laugh. 'Damn the bosses,' she would shout when she had to exert herself more than usual.

'I've nothing against you Possanza, you and we work together. It's those real bosses, those who won't come anywhere near us. And it's those who serve them . . . police, judges, lawyers. I can't stomach all those speeches on the radio. They frighten me, they fill the cities with big words and hatred. And while they rant and rave, we have to eat like paupers.'

'So when are you coming?' She asked. 'Come on Saturday evening, my door's at the top of Fossombrone, via della Cesana, 32. Next to my door, on the wall, I don't know why, there's a bright blue brick. I don't know why. Come on Saturday, after seven. My husband will be gone by then, by that time on a Saturday. He's already drunk by lunchtime. On Saturday he goes and sleeps in the corridors of the cathedral, to guard the treasury, so he says, or be ready to serve at Mass in the morning. Then he digs the bishop's garden, waters his flowers and vases, checks if the figs are ripe and kisses his ring. But when it's time to eat he's packed off to the kitchen. He comes back on Monday evening all being well. Tuesday he goes selling roast pork in Fermignano, Wednesday he's off to Fano market with the cloth merchants. Thursday he stays down there with the fishmonger. Friday morning he comes by here for a while on his way to sell fried fish up in Aqualagna. Friday evening he's back home, well sozzled on a bottle of grappa that he buys up there, bootleg, and drinks half. Saturday morning he pours out the rest, drop by drop, into his coffee and in that way he's just about ready for the bishop. And to think he was one of the best pork butchers in the province.

'And a good accordion player too. That's how he got me, in fact, with his squeeze box, drop by drop like his flask of grappa . . . *Tango delle Rose, Tango del Mare.* You needn't worry, come on Saturday evening. And then, if my husband suddenly turns up, we'll give him a good hiding and lock him in the wardrobe till Monday evening. Perhaps he'll bring a kilo of roast pork for us to eat, with the orange peel he puts in.'

Damìn kept continually checking his knees and his belt, and spent whole hours at the window with each hand gripped around the other wrist. He looked down at his shoes and recognized his shape in them, the distinct lines that converged towards their exact identity; inside were his feet: in a certain way they were not there, and only at night in bed could he feel them free and naked. And to take full possession of himself he would begin to stroke his dick.

His body then was all one, complete and sealed by contentment and by a total sense of guilt that could never be dislodged by any urge or freedom, since it established a condition that he shared with his mother, with the same source and amount of oxygen to continue. And so on, for the four whole remaining days before seven o'clock on Saturday evening. At home, at that hour, they still hadn't eaten, so he invented a story about having to stay out late with other athletes to watch a documentary film.

HE SPENT THE WHOLE AFTERNOON at the cinema and left only just before the arranged time. He hurried up to the top of the town, continually looking for signs in everything and relying on countless omens, marks on walls, pebbles, holes in the cobbles, lizards, tufts of grass. At the top, he stopped under a fig tree that grew out from the wall of the fortress. Nearby was an iron grating inside which was a dark and derelict vault, abandoned for years. He was afraid and felt tempted to go home.

And yet this test was a fateful duty he could not relinquish: the fig tree itself was telling him of the naturalness of that obligation. Could that tree ever suddenly vanish with all its leaves and branches? How did its roots feed among the rocks and such little soil? At seven o'clock he was at the door of No. 32 that overlooked the light-blue brick.

The room he entered was windowless; its light came from the door or from the light bulb that hung high up, or from a fire that must have often been lit, judging from the lingering smell. The woman appeared immediately at the top of the stairs and the light behind her illuminated the large fireplace at the entrance. Damìn was told to close the door and go upstairs, encouraged step by step by the woman's voice: 'What a treasure you are,' she said, 'precious as the oracle. You're so handsome—handsome and sturdy as a tabernacle.'

The woman had combed her hair differently and powdered her face and neck, with a dark, straight, clinging dress that had a white lace collar over a thin gold chain. This collar was the focus of Damìn's attention, anxious already about the task of unbuttoning it.

Lena smiled, with all her curls radiating, her red lips, with no make-up, opened by a smile that did not expose her gums, but with a long row of white teeth all well in line.

She invited him to sit down and have coffee; there was a small white flowery cloth on the table and at the centre a porcelain cat washing its face with its paw. The woman began to smile and Damìn felt more relaxed and comfortable in such surroundings, eased by her laughter. They drank coffee in two small turquoise cups, transparent between the woman's dark fingers; Damìn was worried about how to hold the cup and place it properly on the saucer, but Lena took it away; she took hold of him and went at him with her whole face, to kiss him on the mouth. Her kiss was heavy, clean though moist. She stopped in what seemed to him an appropriate moment, ending it well, without her taking any other liberty—to see, to take a breath.

The second kiss came from Damìn, who also managed to put a hand, and then his whole arm, on the woman's back.

'You don't take me for a whore, do you?'

It seemed to Damìn as though these words had come from her curls and her forehead.

'You don't think badly of me, do you, even though I've asked you into my house? You don't think badly of me, do you? Young people today are educated, they know how to see these things in the right way, no? Love is always beautiful, like a beautiful day, and it's always proper if it's done right, no?'

These phrases echoed intermittently like a poem recited in a happy schoolroom. Damìn was encouraged by them: it was a challenge that seemed possible. Their kiss was now moister, through parted lips. His two friends the runners would already have been there, ready to pounce, with their goading and their swerving. They would already be hunting around below, for hair. After a short pause, Lena opened her mouth and pushed her tongue forward, gently but firmly. Damìn felt completely overwhelmed by a warm organ that seemed much larger than a tongue. He was frightened at the prospect of its taste and that its contact might bring a sudden feeling of disgust. Yet he managed to continue, stirred by a pleasure he had never before experienced. He tried then to savour the ways and depths of that kiss, even introducing his own variations and initiatives. The woman moaned and bent back, almost as if to move away; but he insisted, now happy as much as sure and capable.

They went on kissing for a long while, their whole faces and necks red, their mouths sore. Damìn was gripped by a delight that crossed his whole mind. He forgot about his test, its stages or its completion; nor could he feel his hands any longer, nor any other part of his body. All of his senses were being drawn into his mouth, into his kiss, or flowing and lingering over the woman's face and neck, over those humps and crevices

of flesh down to the root and into the dense and pen-
etrating mass of curls.

He was gaining confidence and pleasure in his
kissing, which had now become a splendid and succu-
lent banquet, to be ever repeated and never eaten. He
thought with warmth and appreciation about those
kisses in the films he had generally scorned, and many
actresses came back into his imagination, ones he had
disregarded until then—those smothered in kisses, faces
that filled the whole screen, bathed by a languor that
to him seemed impossible, excessively ostentatious.

After more than two hours of kissing, Lena struggled free and held on to the table to catch her breath.
She raised her head, over her lace collar, still neatly buttoned, looked across at Damìn, and said: 'Shall we try
doing something else? My room is across there.'

Damìn didn't want to stop and threw himself back
on her, as though he hadn't heard what she had said—
back all over the woman's face to continue his pleasure,
mingled with a frenzy that could be dissolved only in
the liquidity and the keenness of his kiss. Lena
responded, then pushed herself away.

'Enough of this Communion. Enough sighing and
kissing . . . it's too much . . . too much kid's stuff . . . we
can go across there and stretch ourselves out on the
bed.'

Damìn found her words and her manner vulgar and offensive, even obscene.

'Don't say it like that, don't talk like you really are a whore. Straight to bed . . . straight on to business . . . that's what you are.'

Lena said nothing but stared at him. She settled herself down on the chair to collect her thoughts. 'Sorry. Sorry, perhaps I'm wrong . . . since I don't know you. Tell me what you want . . . I'll try to do whatever you say.'

'It's not the same any longer. You've spoilt it all—with your talk and your whorish ways.'

'But no, no. Come here. Come here, you fine big boy, come here, let me hug and kiss you just as you wish. We'll do just what you say . . . no more talking . . . we'll kiss and hug all night long, and tomorrow, standing up or sitting at the table or on the ottoman, however you like it best . . . like two children.'

But Damìn was still smouldering with indignation.

'If you like, I'll put my head against the ottoman so you can kiss me better. Then, gently-gently, if you like, if you let me, I'll touch a little bit, here and there, I'll touch you little by little. But I'll never stop kissing you . . . ever . . . until you want to do something else . . . '

'What else? Now you've spoilt it.'

'Well then, we can start kissing all over again. We'll do everything as you want it. Tell me and I'll do just what you say. Meanwhile shall we have another coffee? Isn't your mouth sore? And in the meantime can I undo my collar, and perhaps slip off my dress? Wouldn't you prefer to kiss me just in my underslip? Why don't you try taking your jersey off as well? You could kiss me better. If you take off my dress you could kiss me further down, on the neck down to the breast . . . Women like being kissed on the breast and men like doing it as well. You just try, gently–gently, and maybe then I can touch you . . . '

Damìn remained immobile, and this also encouraged Lena to continue with her lesson.

'I can touch you while you kiss me. Maybe I can go further down as well, and kiss you on the chest . . . then if you like, still kissing you, I can touch you in front, on your trousers . . . and undo them as well, if you like, gently–gently . . . maybe one button at a time . . . if you like . . . until . . . '

Damìn listened grimly, having lost the magic of her kisses, the pleasure he had felt and, above all, the keenness with which he had received them and returned them each time anew. That woman now continued to threaten him with her words and with those impossible and crazy ideas. He was disgusted and afraid. His fear didn't grow as it usually did, in equal proportion, but spread until it buried him, taking his breath away. His stomach hardened and his breathing too became hard, impossible—with an iron circle around his chest and hands, his neck, around his whole body, everywhere.

'Stop. Stop, stop, that's enough. I've got to go. Open the door, the windows. Whores aren't what I want. They disgust me. They suffocate me. With their fancy words, they go down straight on top of you, no escape. No, no. Stop. Stop, I have to go. I have to get out.'

He was pale and furious, his eyes gazing blankly at the ceiling, his hands thumping the table, independently, incoherent and heavy.

Lena hurried across to open the door and the windows: then all she could think was to fetch a glass of water for the boy who was sick. She could see he really was sick and her instinct told her to make sure he was all in one piece inside that body and clothing of his, that some part of him wasn't missing. He hadn't even shown the curiosity of a boy or the warm bashfulness of an adolescent. He had seemed instead like a body that had neither discretion nor taste—a kind of timeless and powerless machine. He was encased, she thought, like a sapling; like a sapling that couldn't manage even to send out and support a leaf, his hands; with the whole of his head bound up, like a sapling . . . even his face inside its bark, like an elm.

Lena felt pity, but also disgust, and no part of that body now reminded her of the fine youth he had seemed when he first appeared in the potter's yard.

She used much caution and compassion to calm him down and bring him gradually back to himself, having reached the conclusion that he was a poor unhappy cripple, that something must be missing in that inscrutable head of his. She imagined a burnt-out light bulb between two others that were lit on either side, or a switch that had worked itself loose and could no longer connect the light bulb to the other parts of that sad circuit.

DAMÌN WENT BACK HOME furious and devastated, more bitter than ever about the woman and her lust; but he found some reason for consolation, imaging his own superiority towards the vulgar, base and loathsome practice of sex. Yet he feared this terrible experience would haunt him for ever, lying still, beneath the sheets, looking into the empty space to the left, where the ceiling was lower.

The form of that space was colder and colder, and in that coldness it seemed to draw the outline of his fear. It would have been better to carry on ignoring it, to avoid having to recall it for ever.

He turned the other way and tried to make himself comfortable, with his head down on his chest and knees hunched up. In this way he could slip back into the usual mechanism, with his hands back clasping his dick, stroking it until he felt it grow, and could then drift away into pleasure—pleasure with the prospect of new anticipation. Jerking off would cut many of the ropes that held him back: and in doing so, he pictured Lena washing her naked thighs at the pump in the pottery yard, and then, with new confidence, pride and pleasure, he remembered too the kisses he had given her.

Next day he avoided the pottery. He went up to the piazza in search of company. At the kiosk he bought an album of *Tim Tyler's Luck* and *Queen Loana*.

The chaste queen, the ageless and sexless sovereign, half-naked goddess of beauty but impervious to all. In the story in that same album the queen yielded to the love of an explorer escaping from his vain realm of shadows. Luana betrayed him as well . . . Luana the whorish queen. He went to the bookshop to find some adventure story that might raise his spirits, or a book on sports to help improve his physical fitness, and with new recommendations appropriate both for javelin throwing and how to get higher up that wooden score board and overcome the fear that was compromising his distance and preventing him from throwing fast and smoothly. His running friends went running also to get about, to reach somewhere new.

XVI

The State Institute of Art and Book Illustration.
His Mother's City. The Confession. Statues

AROUND MID-SEPTEMBER, with his grandfather's agreement, Damìn decided to enrol at the State Institute of
Art and Book Illustration in Urbino—a well-known
high school, with workshops and practical courses
including pottery, from which many famous artists had
graduated.

On the first day of school he arrived with all the
textbooks, his box of pencils and colours. He was
wearing a new jersey with a large pocket at the back
that could conveniently hold anything that might be
useful for his lessons. He was desperate to understand
and to learn, to discover new things. There were sixteen
pupils in the class, with five girls, all more mature, who
even wore make-up. The most eye-catching brunette
had high heels and lipstick; she lived and moved in her
own light, her bottom clothed and illuminated like a
theatre stage.

After a nerve-racking first morning spent watching
and listening, Damìn left the institute and went to
get his lunch pack, which he had hidden among the
holes of a wall along an alley not far away. He was
embarrassed to go to the school carrying something so

rural and domestic, but now it revived his sense of comfort.

In the afternoon, when lessons resumed, his test involved drawing the plaster cast of a Greek statue: Laocoön and his sons strangled by serpents. To him it seemed the serpent was emerging from the limbs of the desperate old man.

With his pencil he followed rapidly behind the curves of the great composition as though its line might lead him towards some discovery of his own: he worked away on the men's arms and limbs, then moved along with pleasure behind the relentless whirling coils of the avenging reptiles.

The whole great institute, with its immense white spaces, punctuated by tall, empty windows, was crammed with plaster statues in every classroom and corridor, copies of Greek statues of philosophers, athletes, and gods and goddesses with great eyes, colossal heads with beards or helmets, mythological groups in which the protagonists were each present, represented by the symbol of some evil, of some infirmity or wrong. The whole institute, its classrooms and statues, bore the enormity and whiteness of Damìn's pain faintly in the dust; it had that same clammy odour as his groin, and the same mitigating rapture, as impenetrable as that which frequently enveloped his body. The only way of moving in such surroundings was by drawing.

AT THE INSTITUTE HE COULD SPEND whole mornings and afternoons without resorting to the idea or consolation of masturbation: drawing was enough; copying statues or inventing various types of bird, alive on a branch, or dead, laid out in their plumage; or imagining the bends and currents of an African river, of a territory still virgin, with no explorers or queens. But he was also good at drawing the faces of fellow students more agile and lively, more mature and solitary. Many of the students were outsiders, many came from faraway cities like Milan and Naples, and two even from abroad, from Switzerland and Egypt.

His talent was soon recognized. The teachers were diffident at first, but then they had to recognize his consistency and were prepared to view him with more admiration than curiosity. One of the teachers from Milan who taught decorative design became an admirer and enthusiastic collector of his drawings and offered him extra tuition. Before the end of the first term he asked to meet Damìn's parents to tell them how promising he was and to discuss his future with them.

On the appointed day his mother went with him to Urbino. Damìn was happy though embarrassed to see her beside him in the compartment that he now considered external to his family surroundings, disturbed more by the restlessness among student passengers than the speed of the train.

His mother was well dressed and smiled calmly, unperturbed by what was going on. After the last tunnel before Urbino she stood up, went to the window and remained there, as she normally did at the window onto the garden, looking at the countryside still in the grip of winter. She showed no sign of curiosity when the walls of Urbino came into sight. The thought of Marcacci must have been weighing upon her, pushing other things aside.

In the bus from the station she was brighter and more enthusiastic: she was returning to her city, the city she had left as a child before the age of ten after the death of her mother. She remembered those steep descents: the same landscape but, unlike now, it had been all downhill, constantly jolting at such speed that she couldn't see a thing, prevented from fixing any sequence of images in her mind. She was descending, and that was all—always down, down in fast descent to Fano, to an institution run by nuns. She had no chance to stop and catch her breath until she had reached the small inner door to the courtyard of the convent. She would spend another ten years in that courtyard, praying and embroidering, playing blind man's buff and making biscuits for feast days. Biscuits for the convent superiors and benefactors. She was happy even for this, pleased to imagine how tasty they were and how heartily they must have been enjoyed by the happy, fortunate families who received them. She berated another girl who spat into the mixture out of bitterness when she thought no one was looking. She too had a particular quirk: she never wanted to be caught when they played blind man's buff, and if anyone tagged her and made her prisoner she would have a temper tantrum and spoil the game for everyone. If the other girl then kept hold of her, she would drop to the floor feeling nauseous and even faint.

Damìn's mother was chattering away, unusually loudly and lively, with no concern about other passengers overhearing.

At a cafe in Urbino, as they waited, sitting at a table in the main hall, she continued her story up to the day when the man who would become her husband, Dorino, his father, appeared for the first time at that same convent door at which she had arrived after her precipitous departure, when she had stood counting its nails and its studs while she caught her breath. Her shyness and confusion led her back to those same nails and studs, and this time she could see the way they had been formed and the embossed pattern that they made—just like a grille, like a fortress.

Fortunately for her, that door was about to open. She agreed to marry him, returned to the courtyard in great excitement and began running about asking the others, now all grown up, to play blind man's buff once more.

'THIS MORNING I'M HAPPY AGAIN, here with you. Very. Happy to be going with you to school, but also to be with you, together in this city. As though we are free together.'

At these words she stopped, worried that Damìn might wrongly interpret them, but also because they pointed to some inner thought that went beyond their innocent intent. Having realized this, she added hurriedly, in a more insistent tone: 'And we'll go back home together this evening.'

'You're not so happy,' ventured Damìn.

'Why? Not everyone has two clever children, a family and a nice house.'

'But that's not everything.'

'Everything? What is everything? Who can have everything? Those who want everything will never be happy.'

'Everything is simple,' said Damìn, who could easily hurt his mother when the chance arose, 'it means money, a woman to cook and clean . . . writing and receiving letters . . . love.'

His mother fell silent, looking down into her cappuccino. Damìn enjoyed the harm he had inflicted, along with the guilt that it rekindled and which grew inside him.

At the institute, Damìn took his mother along the corridor as far as the first room, leaving her to wait by the plaster group of the Laocoön.

The teacher was most courteous and complimentary. He said they should all be pleased about Damìn's talent and should do their utmost to help and encourage his fine skill in drawing, until the time when he could make a name for himself outside the school, as an artist in his own right.

Damìn listened. This time it was happiness that was urging him to wonder whether the teacher had noticed his mother's beauty—a beauty that had not slipped the attention of the older students, who kept passing back and forth, ever closer to the Laocoön, nor that of the head janitor, the lecherous Cartoceti, who would lurk by the girls' toilets and make blatant attempts to seduce the older ones, or any female student who happened to approach alone.

DURING THE BREAK, Damìn found his mother in the same place, with the janitor nearby, almost next to her, full of courtesies and suggesting she ate at a trattoria by the law courts, where he too would be going for lunch as soon as he was free.

Damìn was offended by these propositions, to the point of disgust. He wanted to challenge this slimy lothario as well as putting his mother to the test; she seemed irritated, though she might simply have been embarrassed by the impertinence, and hesitant out of convenience, or perhaps just playing hard to get.

In reality Damìn was duelling with himself. Once again he was gripped by his own pain. He told her that the restaurant the janitor had suggested was indeed good and cheap.

Through lunch he watched his mother's expression and waited for the janitor to arrive, holding back his anger in expectation of what might have been the final scene of his suffering. In his confusion he had spotted a large butcher's knife on the kitchen hatch through which the dishes were served. If his mother were to yield through some fickle and indulgent force, or perhaps some uncontainable whorish malice, he could grab the weapon and take his revenge, using it even against himself. He kept wondering which of the two he would have stabbed first, and in that uncertainty he shifted and divided his anxiety to help him deal with the wait, to stop himself collapsing to the floor before it happened, as he had begun to fear. Over his body, sprawled across the tiled floor, consumed by misery, the two of them could then embrace with impunity. So he had to wait, preparing the venom, like a viper before it launches its attack.

The janitor arrived without his apron, his hands and wrists shiny with the brilliantine he had smeared across his hair and onto his ears. His advances were insistent and of every kind, as Damìn had imagined. He could feel the movement of the man's feet over the tiles, attempting to touch those of his mother. She had to pull back from the table with her legs bent towards her son. Unperturbed, the janitor ordered spumante and desserts, still laughing and talking.

Soon he reminded Damìn, whose fury was turning into pain and renewed pity for his mother, that it was time for him to go back to school. The boy rose suddenly, shaking. His mother immediately did the same and gave him her hand to follow him out. She left with her son, despite the head janitor's pleas and entreaties, and accompanied him as far as the entrance to the institute. The janitor remained, smiling and greasy, to eat his desserts and drink his spumante.

DAMÌN HAD WON, WITH HIS MOTHER OBEDIENT; yet he couldn't be happy. He calculated to what extent the pain inside him had now grown—driving him to murder. With a horror even more painful for the weight of yearning that overwhelmed and confused him, he thought of all the happiness he might have had, equal and identical indeed to life itself, if his mother had never met Marcacci, if she had not been destroyed by that triumphant bully and snatched away for ever.

And yet an enduring love enabled him, beneath all those traces, strokes, accumulations of that painful truth, to turn and smile at his mother.

The white entrance to the institute marked a line of separation that seemed impossible for him to cross; beyond it, among the statues and white dust he would forever lose his mother and he himself would be transformed into the voiceless plaster cast of an eternal other, a vain figure of pain. She consoled him, saying she would be waiting nearby, in the cathedral, at the far end of the right nave, immediately after she had been back to look at the frontage of the house where she had been born.

Damìn could then enter, and he made his way towards the drawing class and the whiteness of the Laocoön, straining the plaster of his own chest. His hands came to his aid, and he drew nonstop for an hour: the statue of himself, bent over himself, with and without the javelin, his stomach and neck wounded, an arm missing, unsteady on broken, detached feet, marked by the line of a fracture on the ankle of one leg and on the shin of the other.

After the first hour he could hold back no longer and ran to the cathedral. It was vast and empty, with a few lone lit candles that dripped wax. He stood waiting by the largest of them. He couldn't be sure how much of that candle had burnt down by the time his mother arrived. They didn't speak, as if through respect for the sanctity of the place, which they tried also to emphasize by looking up and around. But soon they left and headed down together towards the lower piazza. They walked hurriedly, though there were still two hours before the train went. They moved quickly to avoid having to talk. They went back to the cafe of that morning, and sat at the same table.

'I'M PLEASED YOU'RE DOING WELL,' his mother managed quietly to say at last.

Damìn smiled.

'So clever as to impress the teachers. So clever as to become an artist. You deserve it because you're good. Thanks also to your grandfather—he's an artist as well, even though he's still making pots . . . a true artist. Just think how pleased he'll be. The D.P. mark carries on— it carries on in art, as the teacher said.'

'But I'll be leaving Fossombrone,' said Damìn, 'as soon as I can. As soon as I'm old enough. I can't bear it any longer. Luckily this school . . . otherwise I'd have gone long ago. Fossombrone is throttling me. And it's even worse at home.'

'Why do you want to leave? What's throttling you?' She hesitated in her question but her genuine sorrow compelled her to speak. 'You can go away of course, when you're old enough, to work. And that will only be right, though difficult to accept. A time always comes when children unfortunately have to leave their parents. Especially in the small towns, and especially when the children are clever and have worked hard.'

'Have you ever left us?' asked Damìn.

'I? Left? Why? When would I have left you?'

Damìn gripped the table and peered down, as if to study his legs.

'Have I ever given you the idea I would have left you? I? Left you, you and Lavinia? Wherever would I have gone?'

Damìn continued to grapple with the table.

'But could you really have imagined I would have left you. And could you really have suffered over such an idea?'

Damìn looked up again.

'Haven't I been with you all the time? Every day every moment?'

Damìn let go of the table and giving out a sigh like a long puff of steam from an espresso machine, he asked: 'And at night?'

His mother was shocked but carried on as though she hadn't heard: 'If I was silent sometimes . . . wrapped in my own thoughts. I certainly had no plans about leaving you. Everyone has their own thoughts. Even mothers can have their own thoughts, even sorrows, even upsets—but never against their children, nor ever for a moment with the idea of leaving them . . . ' And she stopped, as if now caught up in some other thought, of a seriousness much greater than what she herself had said, that had been prompted by her son's words.

Damìn, his head upright, and with another long sigh like a coffee machine, said no more, aware at this point that his silence was more painful than any words.

'I have suffered . . . I have suffered much. I might have cut myself off, been a little withdrawn. But I never gave up. I never forgot you.'

Damìn kept a deliberate silence.

'I may also have sinned. Yes. But never has it even entered my mind to do you any wrong or ever to leave you—never for any reason. Not even the worst sin has ever separated me from you. And not even . . . '

AT THIS HESITATION, Damìn turned and fixed his mother in the eye. He understood the fullness of the confession he had managed to extract, and now measured his pride in the intensity of suffering it must have caused his mother to express it. He was so proud that this time his sense of guilt took longer to take a grip. He could even smile, with an attitude of clemency. He crowned his generosity by suggesting they should go, also to save his mother from this place and the situation into which she had been forced, under his attacks, to admit to her own infidelity.

He took her to see the cinema posters and then the windows of the larger shops, particularly those with women's fashions and perfumery.

'Urbino hasn't progressed much,' his mother could say as they reached the bus stop between the pillars of the shorter portico. Damìn now stood beside her brimming with love, his mind freed by her humiliation, by the melancholy within which her own feelings as a mother must certainly now be more solid and determined.

In the golden light of sunset the city relaxed inside its symmetry, serene and solemn in every street and piazza. Damìn was struck by the strong resemblance he found between each building, its light and its beauty, and the face and figure of his mother: the same demeanour and the same calm breath of light and movement. His mother was as beautiful and noble as Urbino, as that city brimming with age and history and yet open and alive. Here too, tyrants and potentates had passed; it too had been invaded and conquered by rival powers. The scenes and marks of their violence and destruction must still have been there—even though the light bathed everything in the same beauty, and remained, once the sun had set, as if it radiated from the very surfaces that it touched.

He walked and watched his mother in the same way, while her guilt continued to exist within her beauty, within the tidy dimensions of her figure.

The light grew whiter, as if to follow the remorse that now re-emerged in Damìn's breast. He tried to hold on to that whiteness so as not to be swept away once more by the waves of his truth: so that he could stop before reaching the usual, inexorable storm of punitive and painful associations.

In the white light, with everything around almost gone, he and his mother, standing still in the narrowest corner of the piazza, could be mistaken for a white statue, a plaster cast from the institute—new and among the most beautiful.

They had the same whiteness and the same fixity and were standing complete in the same light and nothing could ever have changed their form, not even by splitting and separating them—or could ever have torn them from that composition.

On the return journey Damìn was soon distracted from the enchantment of the statue: all the men in the carriage were trying to approach his mother and chat to her, even the railwayman.

XVII

Drawing. Caminito

THAT EVENING AT HOME he held Vitina tight in a long tango and kept holding her, dancing even when the music had stopped. Vitina wriggled out of his clutch, so he went and tapped the beat of the tango on the panes of the window overlooking the garden, following the outlines of its mist and vapour: he could still sound the mellow violin of his thoughts by scratching the frost on the window.

Next day he began drawing Occhialini's workshop with all the details of its equipment and shoes, and with the cobbler at the centre, sitting at his workbench, his arms stretched out from each side of his apron, with his hammer in his right hand; in his left, instead of his skiving knife, a sickle. Occhialini was laughing with his mouth open, and on his lips the letter *p*, the first letter of his favourite definition of the Duce, puppet of the bourgeoisie.

On another sheet of paper he drew himself sitting on the steps of that same workshop, silent, head bowed, with a look of inner confusion, clutching his knees.

Over the next few days he drew a portrait from memory of his mother in her dressing gown, standing open-armed, with her face leaning forward as if to take hold of someone: under her bare feet was the beaten ground of the ruined tower and, nearby, an open space indicated by various pearl-white colours, in its own light. It was marked, liked the ground itself, with mysterious objects, snail and snake trails, small heaps of foul, slimy matter. The open space was reflected in a large oval mirror, similar to that of her bedroom but larger, more nobly framed with acanthus leaves and other classical ornaments like those worn around the heads of great proud and angry statues of goddesses. A large moveable mirror, held and manipulated by a cupid, by a boy . . . by an athlete . . . by an Olympian javelin thrower.

HE THEN DREW HIS MOTHER with her naked breast half protruding from the folds of her dress, a peplos, imitating a benign and languid Flora or Ceres, dispenser of flowers, but also of a great thirst for milk and for food to chew.

Then, on a double sheet, he drew Marcacci, standing in his white colonial uniform, his hands on his hips and dagger in his belt—the murderous dagger with its mother-of-pearl handle.

On another sheet he drew from memory, in meticulous detail, almost to its natural size, the new Abyssinian dagger, the deadly weapon that already held along its blade all the contagion of its victims and of the Ras' bloody hands from which it had been wrenched.

Rapt in his own enthusiasm he drew a portrait of his grandfather, half-length, with all his curls, strong nose, moustache, his neckerchief with its knot held by the Roman cameo. He drew a naked female statue of Diana, dignified and aloof, with a childish swelling at her breast, a finger brushing hurriedly over her groin.

Onto this nude he tried to attach Lena's stern face. He had to add curls and necklaces and then a large ravaged mouth, whose dark corolla was filled by the froth of a monstrous tongue.

He was never able to focus his thoughts and decide how to draw Vitina.

Then, after another series of failed attempts, he sketched two dancers clasping each other in a tango—foreshortened, the figure of the woman falling back in abandonment to the languid lilt of an accordion. The composition was seen from the viewpoint of a musician, with the neck of a violin that jutted out; at the far end, the fingers arranged on the notes and the bow bent ready to launch into the excitement of the main theme. But this was already stretching beyond the sheet of paper, which confused the identities of the dancers and banished every other truth.

IN MAY 1938, DAMÌN HAD TO GO to Pesaro to represent the school in what were known as the Lictorial Games, which included a drawing competition.

The set piece was: a speech by the Duce.

Each competitor also had to produce two freehand drawings: a composition and a landscape, and in the second of these there had to be a scene involving Fascist labour.

Damìn began with the set theme and drew the interior of a farmhouse, with a radio on a mantelpiece, next to a crucifix and a picture of Saint Anthony blessing the animals. The farmer and his wife were sitting at a table, looking towards the radio, listening; others were standing by the fireplace. The man was deep in thought, his hands clutching the handle of a hoe. The whole hoe, in its outline and its shading, was drawn carefully in all its detail, by his feet. The children behind were caught in an attitude divorced from anything real in the room, or any relationship with those present. The grandparents were sitting beside the fire, bent by poverty. At the far end of the kitchen, behind the door, Damìn drew the latest model of a light machine-gun, of polished steel, with handle and stock ready, indeed prehensile against the grain of the timber.

The weapon was loaded, alone and pristine, in the place where a dog might have been, more indifferent than any animal.

The radio and the gun were drawn in the same manner, in a style that was different to any other figure and detail. Damìn was absorbed by the fierceness of the machine-gun, and then, following his continual swings of mood, by compassion: on the table in the middle he drew two loaves of bread, cutlery and dishes, and a wine jug, one of the finest his grandfather had ever made, and clearly visible below the leaf of the decoration, the monogram with the D. and the P. intertwined.

The farmer and his family had to appear inside his reality, clearly declared and circumscribed by the drawing; but struck by the new truth introduced by the radio and by the light machine-gun, they were ready for change and to move forward according to the new order that the radio and the gun proclaimed. Their expectation, still hesitant though eager, was the same as Damìn's expectation of emerging from himself and from his world.

FOR THE COMPOSITION, HE DREW his mother sitting at a loom on which the outline of the warp took the form of a large cobweb. The female figure was dressed in classical costume, with wide drapes, her arms moving in time with her work, one of her hands on the loom

and one on the thread, and her bare feet beneath the
dress distinct and distant from each other in keeping
with the solemn measure of the composition. The focus
of the woman's gaze went beyond her weaving,
prompted by a visible suffering over her whole face,
suffused by the majesty of a adverse fate.

IN THE THIRD PICTURE HE DREW an Apennine valley
torn by bad weather at the end of winter: at the centre,
beside the banks of a mountain torrent, a road was
under construction. A sheer cliff was preventing its
progress and workmen were battling against the rock
with chisels and sledge hammers. In the foreground, on
a concrete construction shelter, Damìn had drawn the
Fascist symbol and had pasted on the door a picture of
the world boxing champion, Primo Carnera, and a
large photograph of the Italian team that had played in
the world football championships in France.

Word soon got around, through a friend of his
teacher who was one of the judges, that Damìn was
likely to win a first, a second and a third prize.

But, though still anxious about the formality of the
competition, he remained quite indifferent about what
would happen to those three drawings which he had
done for others, even though they had touched upon
his own truth.

In the afternoon, waiting at a cafe table for the bus, he drew groups of naked women hunting fawns and some athletes resting, naked too, their muscular limbs stretched out languidly, their heads small and aloof, almost as though lost in the divinity of the game.

Drawing allowed him still to look beyond himself, to endure reality and to understand and preserve it in a way that didn't place him in immediate and bitter conflict with his inner self.

Drawing brought those objects, daily episodes and landscapes under his control, into a conception of himself, in relation to those scenes and objects, that did not, through their usual obstacles and associations, produce new motives for pain, or at least no inducement towards its continual expansion. For this reason he thought of his drawings as real, as an end in themselves, just as substantial, for his hands and for his eyes, as food to be snatched and fought over, to such an extent that he took unkindly to words of praise about their artistic quality or about his talent, and shrugged them off, even with disdain, as soon as they were uttered or repeated by others.

RETURNING BY BUS FROM PESARO, he sketched views of the plain, of the market gardens down by the sea, and then everything inside the bus, from the rear seat where he was sitting, to the driver with his arms on the large steering wheel.

On the front seat, the seat once occupied by Marcacci, he drew himself sitting, holding a javelin high up beside him. Below, beside his own bare feet, he drew a whole series of classical weapons, helmets shields and cuirasses, and the stone head of a young defeated hero.

At home, back in his bedroom, he began drawing another Lena, aggressive and half-dressed, with an inviting smile on her face; beside her he drew a chair with its straw seat broken, and two old shoes beneath. Then he drew a half-naked Lena, with a tangle of cloths over her stomach, stretched out on the bed. Another of Lena completely naked, seen from behind; then Lena dressed as a prostitute, with the same sad face and manner of the weaver he had drawn in Pesaro.

Another of Lena wearing the peplos of a vestal virgin: her hair combed to one side on top, against her neat drapes and the coarseness of her smile that seeped over the virginal composure of her limbs.

He drew an anonymous female nude, about which he managed to indicate with precision only the breasts, pure and solid as a stone capital, a constellation of stars, a verse.

FELLOW STUDENTS, even from the higher classes, came asking for help with their work.

Damìn put everything right for everyone, with no conditions and for no reward; but when the most beautiful girl in the school, the brunette with the theatrical bottom, approached him with a half-finished sheet of paper, he stubbornly refused. She smiled at him, with her painted mouth, her neck tilting coquettishly, showing him the sheet of paper in a manner that he thought was not merely suggestive but indecent. It was impossible for him to look at the paper or let the girl come anyway near him.

He refused in no uncertain terms, shaking his head and almost suffocating in his denial.

And so the rumour spread that Damìn had fallen in love with the girl—the deep, unhappy love that only an artist can feel.

The swift circulation of this rumour, up and up through the whole institute, gave him a keen satisfaction and eventually also a sense of pride in his own talent. Rumours and feelings of satisfaction that extended so far that their circulation, and the pleasure he felt, enabled him to go up to her and help her through a crucial exam test.

Being close to her and her renowned beauty brought Damìn a feeling of contentment, indeed excitement; and yet he felt the coldness of one who could never find the true favour of that superior queen—and he felt self-consciousness, as well as the enormity of the legend that weighed on the unhappy love of artists.

DURING THAT EXAM TIME he received a letter from
Occhialini, once again from Marseille, dated 8 June
1938: 'Yesterday I watched the Italian team play
Norway. It only won by luck. The Fascists in the Italian
national team were about to lose their heads and the
game, jeered by democratic spectators from the whole
of Europe. They behaved as if at war. Greetings and best
wishes to you, a javelin thrower who should be a true
sportsman and not a mercenary.'

Damìn was scared by those lines written on a postcard sealed inside an envelope.

Continuing to ponder their meaning, he began to
regret he hadn't persevered with his javelin throwing.
But he now regarded the sports field, so flat and wide,
as hostile, as impracticable for the entanglements of his
body and his mind. Occhialini and Marcacci stood on
opposing sides of the field, each sending out conflicting
though friendly signals. Occhialini had gone at a certain
point while Marcacci continued to watch over him.
He watched him even as he undressed and carried on
talking to him, moving ever closer ... his head unbearable, his moustache and his lips warm, indecent—ever
closer and evermore naked.

He went outside and ran down to the river bank,
even at night, to throw stones, one after another, ever
harder, like machinegun fire, at any object and, eventually, at the mysterious and complicit darkness that

could still be pierced, broached on every side, even with no target or purpose.

He came back below the house and began to throw pebbles, then larger stones, against the dark head of the ruined tower: even rocks he had taken from the barrier along the river, built especially to protect the walls of the town.

He was the strongest thrower in the whole world, in the whole of that universal globe beneath the stars and planets that glittered inside the lid of the sky above Fossombrone and its valley. He threw stones against this lid as well, and instinctively felt the noise of at least three of his shots that had fallen inside the town. Beyond the gardens, beyond the parapets of the via Flaminia, onto the roofs and onto the cobbles around the piazza.

HE PASSED HIS EXAM with excellent marks and much praise. He promised to continue his drawing through the summer holidays and to read the books the teacher from Milan had recommended.

During the first few days he wandered along the river with his sketchpad and his bundle of pencils; but instead of drawing he spent more time throwing stones, uprooting bamboo canes, going for one swim after another at all the deepest and clearest points. One afternoon he put the sketchpad and pencils down on a rock in a clump of reeds in order to cut a long cane, suitable for going round and whipping weeds, perhaps for fishing and for hitting frogs and lizards. He continued on, forgetting all about them. It was a week later that he remembered, and found the pad and pencils in the same place, almost exactly as he had left them; he stared indifferently at the river and greeted it as a faithful and understanding friend that didn't even need his gratitude.

He headed on towards the pottery yard, though worried by the thought of meeting Lena. She too was embarrassed and tried to avoid him.

But when they were suddenly forced to meet, she greeted him, and smiled, and said she had heard what a clever artist he had become. She spoke with a certain awkwardness, with deference, so that Damìn managed to endure the encounter, and even to thank her.

In the yard, Lavinia was crouching down kneading clay, her legs apart, her thighs exposed as far as her knickers. He was offended by her unseemly pose and avoided her, wandering off behind the main kiln, where he could be alone among the piles of reject pots. There, among the pieces, he found more and more new shapes that interested him—parts and channels of a labyrinth that absorbed his whole mind. He picked up two fragments and took them back to the work areas, to those more distant parts, where series of tall jars and larger pots were lined up waiting to be glazed. From those lines he selected the most cracked and distorted examples and took them back to where he had been before. There he had fun smashing them, with a clean blow or by forcing the crack that had formed when the sun had been too strong.

Crossing the yard, he saw his sister standing beside the main pottery wheel; she had now tidied herself up, and the proximity of the old wheel made her once more a source of purity and affection. He ran across to her, not bothering to finish smashing the pots he had chosen. He held her in a long hug, then helped her arrange the lump of clay on the wheel; he let her work the pot while he set about turning the wheel. He stayed with her, looking after her and watching her; only occasionally did he stand to examine the shape, more and more impressed by her skill.

Vitina was moulding a vase that had a new though very simple shape. A vase that could properly be named after her. Did a vase called Vitina already exist? He seemed to remember it was the name used for a small fully glazed pot, with a heavy lid and a high closing rim, suitable for preserving candied fruit and jams, or spices and pickles.

NEXT DAY AROUND NOON, brother and sister were listening to the radio together. They started dancing to the songs. There was also a tango: 'Caminito', an Argentine song, one of their favourites, played by a well-known orchestra.

But halfway through, Vitina wriggled out of her brother's grasp with a gesture of irritation. Damìn felt humiliated under the continuing swell of the music: the violin played the final refrain with sharps and trills that penetrated his despair.

The next song was to the rhythm of a one-step. They usually danced it by jumping about, transforming it into a kind of furlana, a folk dance. Lavinia took hold of her brother again, but he wouldn't dance. Slowly he turned and went off in silence to his room.

He lay gazing at the ceiling, at the figures that formed there in the flow of his pain. Over and again, his eyes traced each brick, each line of mortar, each shadow cast by the beams. He also found new marks: even three old nails on the largest beam, towards the far end, in the shadow; the broad irregular heads of nails made at a time when they were still beaten into shape, one by one, in blacksmiths' forges. Nails of that type were just right for him, fixed here and there into the plank that held him rigid.

He resolved to start painting with oils so that he could recreate an area just like that, solid and bristling with signs and paths; to lay out the material more than its form or size, and to insert iron nails here and there, those at the top driven halfway in, the others, inside the composition, deeper, so as to become almost lost in the material.

A small yet certain truth had finally developed between them. Lena must have been increasingly convinced of it, as though she were passing each day with this young man at work and returning home each evening to gaze again at the portrait. So that two weeks later, having collected her wages, she stopped Damìn and said: 'Why not come back and see me?'

The question was veiled with a certain apprehension and reserve. Damìn spent the next two days pondering the invitation, gripped by an inner conflict into which he threw himself entirely, unreservedly, with no concern about being swept away, or that its power might overflow and become visible from outside, revealing to the whole world how poorly he was made, and how unhappy. Inside the confusion of his impulses he well knew this conflict would determine the whole course of his life.

Meanwhile he watched Lavinia intently writing letters, and it once occurred to him that some of those letters might be addressed to some real living person: one among those groups of boys on bicycles along the via Flaminia, or those tighter and more exclusive cliques that gathered in the piazza and played billiards.

The previous day they had again danced together in a tango, a beautiful Italian song; he had kept his distance and had avoided complicated movements and flourishes. His sister had also been aware of their distance, precise in her gestures, agile in her dance steps, but impatient.

Lena came up to Damìn. 'Why not come back and see me?' she said.

She passed three more times between the vases set out in lines to dry before their bases were trimmed, then she spoke again: 'We can try again. We'll do just what you want.'

That evening in his room, Damìn pulled out a drawing of Lena, one of the larger ones, and re-examined it, line by line. He was studying it formally, though satisfied that certain touches gave an impression of the woman's gaiety, of the confusion in which she lived, or at least the confusion with which she viewed him. But her whole figure lacked warmth and stirred no true desire in him.

Next morning Damìn's mind was full of his plan to meet Lena, each detail of its preparation, his anticipation and repetition of the test, getting to her house, their encounter, his first moves once he was beside her—rehearsed over and again, each time as far as his first gestures: up to the moment of coming to terms with the reality of being with her.

A later part of the film still had to be worked out; on the last time he hadn't known how to prepare for it. The second part had to consist of all the actions, words and movements of his first carnal relationship

XIX

The Battle for Grain. The Country Festa.
Navigare necesse est

AT THE END OF JULY the corn was threshed in the farms of the small district beyond the old bridge to Sant'Ippolito.

Already by midday the noise of preparations and the laughter of the women, particularly the farm girls, could be heard from the potter's yard.

'Sluts,' said Lena. 'All sluts in uniforms. Wearing peasant's headscarves but lots of necklaces. Nicely dressed, but with the bums of sluts. City whores. Station and hotel hookers . . . farmers, ha!'

Damìn's grandfather had laughed and asked her to moderate her language.

When it was time to stop work, the strains of an accordion could be heard among the blasts of a trumpet.

Through the afternoon, people had been passing, many in Fascist uniform; a truck and two motor-vans laden with articles, equipment and timber for the makeshift stage, baskets of food and plates. Four or five whole families of farmers had gone by on their way from the west of Fossombrone, from Calmazzo and the Cesana hills.

All had waved to Possanza and his workers. The last of them had stopped to offer wine.

Lena could drink straight from a jug holding four litres or more, known as a *truffa*, without letting it touch her lips. She lifted it high with both hands, giving Damìn a look of defiance as she poured.

But when she lowered the jug she turned with a lingering eye that betrayed a shy affection, making her blush.

Youngsters from the town also went by, and a group of schoolgirls, some of whom Lavinia knew. Lavinia wanted to go to the festa as well, and begged her brother to hurry back home with her to change. She came out of her room in her best clothes, wearing make-up; Damìn had merely washed his hands, without changing or combing his hair. He went off with Vitina and watched her arrival in the midst of the festa with a joyous smile for everyone, triumphantly joining her circle of friends in her bright blue dress.

He wandered about, not approaching anyone. The orchestra was playing loudly and all were dancing with an enthusiasm that shook the avenue of trees between the lanes and the buildings. The area towards the houses was edged by carts, and tables laden with food, baskets of fruit, plates.

of behaving like everybody else—and his need instead to censure them firmly and even to the point of condemnation.

Meanwhile the farm girls were being hugged and kissed and escorted away; while others ran towards the bushes laughing and not looking back, sure that someone would be following them.

The rounds of drinks and the distribution of food continued; comments and remarks about the abundant harvest, its benefits for those families and for the public good, all part of that general, national Battle for Grain—proclaimed by the Duce, fought and won by every farmer, to everyone's delight and approval in these many celebrations.

Occhialini's European audience would not have understood such revelry, and many would have mocked all of those honest people who offered themselves with such dedication, with their whole body, even with the most flagrant vulgarity and with unbridled shame, displayed even in the great outpouring of public joy. Turning work into a battle, like a game.

Damìn saw everything with the exaggerated tones of the immense, throbbing pain that gripped him. That vase of his felt the violent thrust of a great sharp blade.

OTHER DANCES FOLLOWED, more and more furiously, and then a wild furlana, pushed to fever pitch by the loudest refrain, in which everyone took part, even the older men and women, Fascists and farm workers, townsfolk and labourers—the women all at the centre, tramping repeatedly on their heels, then over and again on their toes; then on one foot and then on the other, turning round and round five or six times in succession to the point of reeling, jostling with one another to keep on their feet, in the dust, with their black skirts over black-stockinged knees, tied roughly at the top with yellow elastic inner tubes; several ribs of their corsets split, many buttons lost to expose their linen blouses beneath, or even skin, in two distinct tones, of those poorer women who didn't even have the intimate comfort of underwear; heels broken, shoes falling apart, slippers split, clogs thrown off, barefooted on the ground—hard, dark, tormented by some unnatural purpose, by some tumult that rocked everything, beyond the poor memories, emaciated limbs and meagre spirits of those wild dancers.

The orchestra lost its rhythm and fell into disarray. Many players climbed down for something to eat and drink, and to find themselves a woman.

The billhook remained firm and shiny in its place, its handle protruding from the stage.

Meanwhile they were serving roast rabbit and stewed goose, with warm flatbread and trays of baked tomato and aubergine.

XX

Beneath the Body of the Murderer

AFTER THREE PIECES JUST FOR ACCORDIONS, the whole orchestra started up again. Damìn was still watching the festivity, following the various groups and studying the way each of them moved about; but he kept an eye on his sister. When the waves of excitement concealed the light-blue aura of her dress, he never lost the exact sense of her position in the midst of the enormous crowd of dancers.

Vitina had danced nonstop, often inside that cyclone; sometimes distinct in her rhythm and movements; preferring the same youth, a boy from the town, tall, with a light shirt. He danced well, always managing to find his way through the tightest vortices. His tall, bright collar helped Damìn keep track of his sister.

He moved closer to watch the boy and noted keenly, in mild alarm, every detail of his figure: the blue–and–white check of his shirt, the large gilt cuf-flinks on the rectangular cuff that covered his wrist and half of his hand. He wore a crocodile–skin belt with sil-ver buckle and baggy, well–ironed trousers of colonial

266

canvas that dropped right down over new brown-and-white brogues.

He must have been from Fossombrone, but a boy who went somewhere else to school and came home for the summer. His curly hair, shiny with brilliantine, tapered low and thick over his collar.

Damìn strained to view his face, and saw sharp expressive features, up to the shadow of his brows, with his eyes constantly looking down at Vitina's head. This prolonged, fixed pose had irritated him, so that he felt obliged then to note a kind of lecherous childishness that crept down his cheeks, giving them a damp tubercular appearance.

This lanky individual, in fact, was breathing heavily, even when he kept his mouth open, with lips pursed, beneath the solemn aspect of two waxed whiskers.

Damìn felt relieved when Vitina moved off to dance with someone else, but this hadn't happened now for several dances.

Then, to control and allay his feeling of alarm, he moved closer to the dancers. His sister still kept her eyes to her partner's creamy gaze, interested in nothing else around. Her face reflected that masculine light, almost fixed to it.

The full moon, suddenly emerging halfway in the sky, made everything more white and hazy.

The moon must now have been shining into the window overlooking the garden, against whose panes his mother, lifting the lace curtains, would almost certainly be resting her head.

THE LANKY YOUTH WAS STILL DEEP in conversation with Lavinia, moving his head in the ingratiating manner of a matinee idol, to seem more alluring and persuasive. Every so often he raised an eyebrow or curled his lip, as if to smile, with an arrogance, who knows with what mark of superiority, with what forwardness. He furthered this seduction by stepping back, and then, as he brought her closer, he bent down to gaze at her, with a look of entrancement, moving both eyebrows, one after the other.

In the tangos, fortunately rare, the tubercular figure stooped forward, holding her close, thrusting his long face beyond Vitina's so that his sharp luminous features mingled with her loose hair.

Vitina's only defence was a taffeta ribbon that tied her hair in a bow behind her neck.

In the tango even her ribbon disappeared beneath the tubercular figure whose sharp nose, lips and chin sank into her hair as far as the back of her neck.

And then he began holding her tightly like this for every dance: for each polka and the succession of waltzes, dancing out of time, in the same slow and seductive way.

Vitina laughed and disappeared even further beneath and within him. During one of those long dances, the youth even managed to wink at a friend who was moving past, dancing to the right tempo—a gesture that surely meant no good.

Damìn managed to hold his rage as the orchestra took a sudden break.

VITINA COULD LEAVE HER PARTNER and smiled across to her brother. Damìn made a brusque and inarticulate gesture—a threat but also a plea, with both arms incoherent with anger and despair.

She approached him but remained silent; she wanted nothing to eat or drink, nor was there anything she wanted to see or hear, nor did she agree that it was time to go home. Damìn tried anxiously to distract her and diffuse the anticipation that gripped her. He was gripped by anger and more so by jealousy. Reflected in his sister's indifference was his own feeling of self-contempt, the extraneousness of his presence from the whole festivity.

He managed to persuade Lavinia to take just one sip of wine, but she wouldn't relax for an instant: she was growing anxious and continually looking about her. The orchestra had started up again; she tapped along in time, swaying with her whole body to a loud and popular rumba, a fairground rumba: 'To the sound of the trumpet, with you my little blonde.' Vitina soon headed back confidently towards her partner as he waited for her, nodding his head, with one hand raised, open. Damìn moved around the edge of the dance floor and in front of the stage, propping his shoulders against the protruding planks.

He felt how his shoulders and the planks came together to form a firm bowstring, seething with energy. He could still feel it quivering, almost urging, with an intensity greater than all the fire and smoke of the festa, greater even than all the fire and smoke of the houses beyond the bridge, and even further away in those inland towns scattered in the darkness of the night. With the same intensity and surging force as the electricity he had heard humming at the Fossombrone substation down the river, which powered the railway station, the hospital, the prison and all the streetlamps along the via Flaminia.

The power of the bowstring grew inside him, no longer under his control. He could feel its vibration, though otherwise he felt confused within his own uncertainty and unhappiness. Yet this time his anger was cold and detached: it held the whole of his blood tight, ready to spill it.

The tubercular figure was still there with Vitina and continued talking and smiling at her, holding her ever tighter. His words must have been a mere accompaniment to the intimacy they now shared. Soon his lust welled up in the proximity of their bodies, in the touching and stroking of legs.

Now it was Vitina who spoke hurriedly, firmly. Her cheeks were red, though her gaze was still clear; and what she was saying must not have been matching his own words, measured by the same worry.

THE DANCE ENDED.

Damìn tried to stir himself, to get up and stand higher to get a better view, but also to breathe and escape, at least as far as his neck, from the grip of that bowstring.

The two dancers had moved slightly apart, waiting to hear the rhythm of the next dance before taking hold of each other again.

Vitina's breast was heaving inside the open neckline of her dress. The trumpet started up with South American whorls and snatches, while a more mellow and nostalgic note continued alone, detached, venturing beyond, further away and deeper down. And so too inside Damìn. Halfway through the trumpet melody, the orchestra erupted with all instruments playing.

The lanky figure glistened as he bent to take hold of his partner. Vitina stepped forward, as if to yield, as though the clothes in which she stood was wanting somehow to remain behind, to hold her back, being more prudent than she, obedient to the teachings of good family decency. Her body slipped away and bent itself with a broad undulation of head and shoulders, as if to strip naked and lie down, yielding to the pleasure, to the subjection of the male. Damìn had seen a perfectly identical gesture: it was the same as that of his mother when she surrendered herself beneath Marcacci; with the same undulation of hair and neck, the same tenderness of her hips as they relaxed. Damìn felt an immediate explosion of the bowstring that shook him, swept away by the anger already inside: to put a stop to that next, inevitable scene, the one he had known and witnessed so many times and imagined still more often, with the body of the woman naked on the ground, beneath the body of the murderer—that of his mother beneath Marcacci's dark limbs and his curls, and now the body of his sister beneath the pallor of that lecherous youth.

With his hand he felt the billhook, there waiting for him, and the whole of his blood surged with the whole force of his body, together with that bestial joy that exploded in the fulfilment of the act; he hurled the blade at Lavinia's neck, the final gesture, as the sinner yielded. The mighty billhook had to cut through everything—every ligament between that body and the images of sin, every internal knot of flesh gripped by guilt.

It had sliced through over three-quarters of the girl's neck, to halfway down her chest, level with the top button of her dress. Lavinia's eyes gouged a white streak across the mass of people, clear as far as those watching far away, sitting on the carts. The youth who was holding her was still supporting her, then gradually accompanied her riven body as it slumped down: face half up, her legs and skirt still tidily arranged, her face bent back, in horror, and because the head had been almost detached by the blow.

In his arm, Damìn could feel the certainty of what he had done and kept hold of the billhook. He struggled free from the spell that fixed his gaze to his lost sister, to her tender chest ripped apart. A bubble of breath and blood that formed instantly deep in the wound brought him to his senses. He ran towards the bridge, cutting behind the orchestra and the straw ricks to slip away from his pursuers and anyone from outside who might have tried to stop him. He ran with that same force with which he had killed Lavinia. The night air of the river touched his lips and his burning brow; along the road he heard the majestic roar of his own impetus, which gave him courage for the final gesture. Without ever slowing down, he arrived halfway along the parapet, and when he recognized the angle in the wall at the point where the road narrows, over the highest arch, he leapt.

HE TRIED TO FIND SOME POISE and inner balance, just like a javelin, so that he would fall as far out into the darkness as he could, behind Vitina, behind the ribbon of her untied bow.

As he passed over the parapet, his momentary yet crystal-clear view of it brought him, for one instant, a dark feeling of nostalgia for that ribbon, for her bow still neatly tied, the image of a sweet truth, for him too, that he had now shattered for ever. The untied ribbon now traced out his path as he launched himself into the darkness. The reality of the void convinced him of the wonder he was about to achieve: with no more pain or regret; with sensual delight, with perfect skill.

XXI

1940. The Majolica Tomb. The Name Damìn.
A Well on the Skyline

OCCHIALINI RETURNED TO FOSSOMBRONE on 1 November 1940 and immediately, on that day of remembrance for the dead, he learnt that his young friend Damìn had thrown himself from the Sant'Ippolito bridge after killing his sister with a billhook. He had thrown himself off with such force that he had crashed against the rocks and pebbles on the other side of the upper rock pool below the bridge, at least twenty metres beyond the parapet. He had flown there, onto the only stretch of bank above water, as though he had calculated the distance. Amilcare was still at the bus stand, holding his suitcases.

The French police had deported him with the approval of the Italian police or perhaps after some specific request. He had spent a few days in Turin, but had chosen to return to Fossombrone, back to his home and his workshop and to see his friends again, also to become more politically active in a place he knew and where he was known. In any event, no one could prevent him from going back to his job.

On that All Saints' Day, two years later, there was still much talk about what had happened to Damìn and his sister and the rest of family. Many commented about the responsibility of the mother and father while others chose to emphasize the role their grandfather played in the whole business in the light of its unexpected conclusion.

By every account Damìn seemed a crazed young man, a lone and sullen artist, jealous of his sister, overwhelmed by a monstrous and uncontrollable athletic force.

The sister was always small and tender, as beautiful as any predestined victim. The guilty mother had immediately withdrawn into desperation and guilt. The father had gone away, though he had already been frequently absent, now estranged from the family. The grandfather had kept a controlling hand over the tragedy. He had comforted and helped his daughter-in-law, perhaps overindulgently and with certain ulterior motives.

He had been to the hospital to collect his grandchildren's corpses as soon as the formalities were complete. He had laid them out together in the same chapel of rest which he himself had filled with flowers, and had then taken them to the cemetery in the same cortege: the two coffins on the same hearse, under the same wreath.

He had followed them alone, in silence, on foot as far as the cemetery, with his black silk scarf loose around his neck, his broad-brimmed hat in his hand.

He had been accompanied by all his workers and, behind them, a few of his grandchildren's friends from the surrounding villages. At the end of the procession, Damìn's drawing teacher, who had come specially from Milan.

At the cemetery Possanza had buried Damìn and Lavinia together, next to each other, on one side of the family chapel, even helping the masons to brick up the graves.

He had then designed a ceramic monument a few weeks later, which he himself had erected over the two graves, midway between one and the other.

NEXT MORNING, ON 2 NOVEMBER, Occhialini went early to the cemetery to visit the tomb of his friend and admirer, and his informer, a sensitive and tragic young boy in a blind society, who was truly worthy of a memorial and a flower, and to visit his sister whom he had taken with him.

The cobbler had also gone to see the work of their grandfather, a fine craftsman with anarchic sympathies.

The family chapel was open and well tended and immediately recognizable with the two graves at the far end, in the floor beside the small altar that had been moved to one side to provide space. To the rear of the two twin slabs, on which were engraved just the names and dates of the brother and sister, there was the stump of a tree, which looked as though it had grown there, out of the ground—in the form of two trunks severed at the base, one slightly larger than the other, joined as though two seeds had grown together with their roots intertwined. They had been severed so that the two trunks formed a single platform, at the far end of which jutted a sliver of roughly cut bark.

This was a tender detail and full of truth.

At the centre of the small platform were two bunches of flowers, one resting on the other: the smaller dependent on the larger one, and some of its leaves and stems entwining into it. The larger bunch was inter-woven with field irises, poppies, wild pinks, ferns and hawthorn leaves, edged with bramble shoots and other prickly foliage. It was neatly arranged into a garland, flower by flower, in a circle of sprigs and greenery; here too, on one side, the flowers seemed ruffled and dishevelled as though caught by a gust of wind. Resting on the other side was the smaller bunch, all violets and primroses, a mass of them—the leaves of one of these growing out beneath the hawthorns of the larger bunch.

All modelled by hand, the trunks and the garlands, each leaf and thorn crafted separately. Each flower, leaf and branch coloured and glazed in many shades; vivid in the distinctive character of each, and as a whole.

The whole work had a clarity and composure in its own humility and in the purpose it served there. It could be recognized in the workmanship and in the materials of the majolica, and perhaps this was why it seemed fitting and serene.

Occhialini was deeply moved and felt an over-whelming sympathy for old Damiano who had made it and who, through working on it, could discharge some part of his terrible grief: to find some meaning to the tragedy. Then, seeing that the weather held good, indeed it was mild for that first autumn of war, he continued on from the cemetery towards the river and across the Sant'Ippolito bridge. He stopped halfway, with a hand on the corner of the parapet, to look down at the current. That surely was the point from which young Possanza had thrown himself after he had killed his sister.

BELOW, THE RIVER FLOWED AS ALWAYS, and to him it seemed unchanged; just the same as when he was a child, perhaps less noisy. He continued on over the bridge, towards the pottery. Peering in through the fence at the far end, he saw Possanza kneeling in the yard beside a heap of clay. He looked much the same, with just the same curls and moustache, and the same deep, slow expression. They greeted each other warmly, and exchanged news and pleasantries.

'We are on this earth,' concluded Damiano after their greetings. 'And always here to work.'

'Purposefully and well. Those who work wisely, skilfully, especially with their hands, will survive once again. Many nations no longer have principles, nor respect for people, especially for those who work. Their ideas are weapons, and their projects are plans for destruction. The popular masses are the only ones who can still think: because they still work with their hands, and because they are afraid.'

In the meantime Norma Possanza, the mother and protagonist in this story, emerged from the main shed, barefoot and wearing a large work coat.

Occhialini greeted her in a loud voice but could find nothing more to say. The woman responded and continued with her work, heading off towards a line of pots laid out to dry.

'She stays with me,' Possanza said, 'works and lives with me. She's very good. Better than me in everything, even when it comes to my own work. She makes the most beautiful pots I've ever seen—new even in their colour and glaze.

'She has a streak of kindness that comes naturally, that keeps on flowing.

'After we left the house in town, sold up to satisfy my son, we had no option but to come here. Less than a month later, one morning she came out and started making a pot. Now she runs half the pottery and does the housekeeping.

'She has a clear idea about everything and never gets lost or sorry for herself. Never forgetful or confused. Nor does she have much to say, not in front of others. She orders and arranges things, and in this way she can work and keep herself going. She can live.

'We're here all the time, together. We live and work here, and sell here direct to customers.'

Norma kept away, not approaching even when the two men said goodbye.

OCCHIALINI PRESSED ON, away from the river, past the first fields, though dusk was falling fast and it was turning cold.

Further ahead were the farmers, the proletarians of the land, those comrades of the class he had to get to know and help; but first he had to recognize himself as one of them.

The rules of the outlawed Communist Party required him to choose a *nom de guerre*. He had to inform the provincial leader at the next meeting. He'd decided to take the name Damìn, in that first step towards the revolution: out of affection for that tragic youth, and because the boy had fallen victim to the bourgeois society.

The evening found him walking among farmland. He seemed to hear footsteps behind. He turned around but could see nothing. He thought perhaps he was being followed and watched, so he stopped. There were sounds in the surrounding hills, now dark. The first house was on the skyline, far away, and glistened with white lime-wash on the walls of its well. That soft horizon, speckled by the great dark oaks at the crossroads and along the boundaries, intimidated him, frightened him, bringing back memories of ancient rituals and the fear of potential ambush. But then he remembered how the whole land of Europe was now encircled by far darker and more threatening powers, traversed and ravaged by the flames of war; and how vast armies of destruction and even whole captive populations were being driven against them.

He set off again towards the white lime-wash of that distant well, no longer frightened, no longer looking back.

Afterword

This novel is, or at least seeks to be, about understanding; even if that understanding is never achieved and its qualities are derived only from the negative of its disasters. [. . .] The launch of the *acontistés* can be followed and measured, but neither extended nor corrected; even less repeated. But inside its parable there ought to be something to be found and understood, if only some cry, a gust of wind, helpful as a broad and modest introduction to the world and to the understanding of young people even of today.

Paolo Volponi[1]

1. *The Javelin Thrower* (*Il lanciatore di giavellotto*), first published in 1981, is an intriguing novel about the experience of pain. It can also be disturbing: Paolo Volponi (1924–94), known as an 'industrial' and 'experimental' writer, has offered his readers a *Bildungsroman* in reverse,

1 This handwritten note appears on four sheets of a notebook entitled 'Studium for Sketches', seen by the writer of this introduction at the author's home in Milan, thanks to Giovina and Caterina Volponi.

transforming the traditional theme of a young boy coming of age into one of pain and desperate alienation. The closely woven plot is centred on a sexual and sentimental education and its bodily sufferings, which are portrayed using a decidedly 'visual', pictorial and cinematographic form of writing. Damìn, the protagonist, might seem a typical early-twentieth-century Italian character, a creation of Federigo Tozzi, Romano Bilenchi or Alberto Moravia—the adolescent who cannot integrate. He is a figure nurtured at European level by Alain-Fournier's *Le Grand Meaulnes* (1913) or Raymond Radiguet's *Le Diable au corps* (1923) or, even more, by a work like Thomas Mann's *Tonio Kröger* (1903), in which the youth's unresolved conflict with reality is determined by the artist's exclusion from society. Yet by the time Volponi's novel was written in the early 1980s, his main character was seemingly fifty years out of his time.

The Javelin Thrower recounts the childhood and adolescence of Damìn Possanza in the central Italian town of Fossombrone during the Fascist years of the 1930s. It is divided into twenty-one numbered chapters, each with headings that give a summary of the action: the use of captions at the beginning of each chapter, unusual for Volponi, is indicative of the author's intention to mark out each episode and to observe the narration from above. But the story is so steeped in pain that something seems destined to slip out of the author's control from the very beginning. Not surprisingly, the title and some of the chapter headings refer to symbols of bloodshed: 'The Javelin', 'The Silver Dagger', 'The Sword of the Rad'. And the title itself is not just descriptive, as indicated by a particular passage, where the headmaster of the school, bizarrely dressed as an army major in the Bersaglieri corps, congratulates Damìn for his record-breaking javelin throw:

> A regional, perhaps a national record. They're waiting for further news and confirmation. The emulation of Homer, classical fervour poured into noble Latin blood. *O acontistés . . .* this is what a javelin thrower is called in Greek. *O acontistés*, which also means thrower of darts, of glances, of desires . . . of ourselves (pp. 148–9).

The javelin in the title therefore alludes to the protagonist's fate. But there are also archaic connotations, as the Greek word suggests, that go back much further than the headmaster's patriotic rhetoric. Apart from this, the themes of Oedipal relationships and incest, as we know, have always been subjects over which hang a vast tragic spectre.

2. The two poles in this novel are the body and history: and this mitigates the sense of disorientation that readers might experience in Volponi's movement back and forth between experimental writing and traditional

storytelling. The theme of the body, indeed, remains central in all of Volponi's writings and in constant tension with social and economic concerns: in his novel *Memoriale* (*My Troubles Began*, 1962), the body of Albino Saluggia and his 'troubles' in the factory; in *La macchina mondiale* (*The Worldwide Machine*, 1965), the body-machine of Anteo Crocioni the peasant farmer and his utopian conjectures; in *Corporale* (1974), the schizoid body of Gerolamo Aspri and his anxieties about nuclear destruction. Here too, in *The Javelin Thrower*, the body and history enter into dialogue and conflict: Damìn's disastrous emotional experience, his grandfather's work as a potter, his father's early enthusiasm for mass production and the media's early promotion of Fascism, all interact, as in a force field.

The representation of human labour, courageously investigated by Volponi from his earliest works, and by a few other Italian writers, such as Primo Levi in *The Wrench* (1978), is also a distinctive feature of *The Javelin Thrower*. It is significant, in this respect, that the story opens from the viewpoint of the grandfather, Damiano Possanza, the 'master craftsman' (p. 6) whose vases, pots, dishes and jugs were admired beyond the boundaries of the province. The unforgettable figure of Norma Coramboni, Damìn's mother (one of the most beautiful, noble and true-to-life women in late-twentieth-century Italian narrative, and all the more eloquent in her silence), is initially filtered through the eyes of the grandfather, who senses the illicit attraction of his daughter-in-law and tries to keep out the 'oppressive truth' through the creative power of work ('He was a master craftsman, almost an artist, and as such he had to make a living and fend for himself' [p. 6]).

The 'call' of desire and the creative 'mastery' applied to the clay, to objects and colours, are the forces that separate the language of *The Javelin Thrower* into two distinct and conflicting metaphoric fields: sexual desire, and civil society. Symbolic order prevails in the first while the second is marked by a cognitive effort: the realm of the home, the garden, the pottery works are represented from the viewpoint of the old craftsman through shapes, light and chromatic qualities ('greyish coil', 'green stain', 'ashen white', [p. 3]) similar to the methods he uses daily in working and moulding the clay. 'Giving form' with his hands and with his mind, observing and describing painful objects and events, ordering and understanding them: this is the ethic that governs the whole novel.

Yet the grandson's destiny is also tragically associated with his grandfather's desire. The name Damìn is a shortening, in regional dialect, of Damiano. The boy is the continuation of the grandfather, the one who 'by family tradition would take his name' (p. 4). When he was born, the old man had planted a fig tree in the garden, and a subtle allusion guides the old man's gaze from the trunk of the fig tree to Norma's 'fancy pink dressing gown'.

Damìn, at the age of nine, is still absorbed in the homely idyll that centres on the figures of his mother and paternal grandfather:

> The centre of his world was the figure of his grandfather, which grew larger and brighter every day. He was strong and tall, malleable, and also useful for better enjoying and exercising his feeling of possession over his mother.
>
> The recurring joy that sustained him in all and everything was his memory of clutching his mother's breast, with one hand thrust between her bosom and the other stretched out to touch his grandfather's face: his mouth and his moustache (pp. 12–13).

His sister Lavinia, called Vitina 'for short, as well for affection' (p. 13), is also a part of that way in which the protagonist engages with the world:

> to the extent that he could lift her up and move her about as he wished, or could cover her with his body and kiss her, or make her cry or laugh, pinch her or hug her, lick her or bite her (p. 12).

His father Dorino, on the other hand, a vague and incomprehensible presence from the very beginning, is the only disturbing element. The extraneousness of the father is another of the constant features in Volponi's writing, a presence that appears in his early poems 'Cugina volpe' ('Precarious paternity / the winter tells me') and 'La vita' ('When I was born / my father wasn't there') and re-emerges in his coming-of-age novel *La strada per Roma*, and in the tragedy of Damìn:

> He could never properly understand where his father was and what he was made of—not even when his father was sitting in front of him at table. There was always something about him and his manner that escaped him, becoming like a sharp line or a heavy ray of light that struck him as it fell (p. 12).

In *The Javelin Thrower*, the fragility of the father is laden with significances that take him from his role as an individual and place him in the historical and social realm of work and production. Dorino is ready to yield to the temptations of Fascism, is prepared to break away from the traditional family business and follow new middle-class myths of easy wealth: for him, pottery will be replaced by aluminium and enamelware, large-scale production has to take the place of craftsmanship.

Damìn cannot identify with his father, not least because, unlike his grandfather, his father sees work not as a creative project but as a means of making quick money. Old Damiano is an artist and a craftsman, continuator of a long popular tradition, whereas Dorino is excited by change and 'innovation' and sets up a makeshift business, buying a lorry so that he can sell new industrially-made tin products from town to town:

'He who stops is lost!' said Possanza ironically.

'And if that were true? And if everything really is changing, the whole of Italy, work, business, industry under Mussolini's great projects? Land reclamation, new cities, asphalt roads, housing projects, schools, sport, transport, hospitals . . . ' (p. 95)

The portrayal of the first steps towards Italian modernization driven by Fascism may well allude to the vaster modernization that would happen later, in the 'miracle' years of the 1960s. Yet here the Italian mass culture of the 1930s, when signs of modernity appeared for the first time, is described with unparalleled effectiveness: Damìn's mind is filled with magazines, popular literature, the comic strips of *L'Avventuroso*, Tarzan, Queen Luana, athletics, touring cinema, exotic stories from the colonies, rural festas.

3. Damìn's paradise is destined to fall apart dramatically. The defining scene drags Damìn into the depths of pain with no possibility of escape. 'Pain' is a narrative motif and a rhythmic and thematic component of this novel in the same way as Albino's 'troubles' in *Memoriale*. The protagonist's fixation is translated into the impossibility of escaping from himself. The metaphor of the 'vase' appears in the text in relation to Damìn's body to portray his incapacity to 'pour himself' into others. While his contemporaries, grouped together, are spying on women at the river or embarking on their first sexual exploits in brothels, he would never be able 'to put on stage any other woman who was not his mother' (p. 42).

Damìn's apprenticeship of destruction is accompanied and overlaid by an explicit persuasive and pedagogical intent on the part of the narrator. As a counterbalance to Damìn's claustrophobic obsessions and dominant sexuality, with the abounding presence of muscles, athletes and brothels, Volponi sows instructive voices of popular reason in the text, vehicles for a moral sexual redemption: first, Amilcare Occhialini, the anti-Fascist cobbler, a sort of 'teacher' for the young of the district; second, Lena, the pottery worker; and third, Damìn's grandfather, Damiano Possanza. The family story of Marcacci the centurion, in Chapter XII, is pervaded by a form of grotesque humour, Volponi's homage to Carlo Emilio Gadda, whose *Eros and Priapo* ridiculed the phallic rites of Fascism. Occhialini's conversations, on the other hand, have an obvious purpose as sexual and political education:

> Women have to get enjoyment like men, and more so, out of social justice and as a reward

for giving birth . . . The skill of a man isn't so
much in how big and hard it is and the number of times he's able to fuck . . . but in the act
of helping and serving a woman, in making
her enjoy it, in having the honesty to enjoy her
fine body . . . all, all of her body (p. 38).

Lena, the pottery worker, also performs the same
instructive role:

You don't think badly of me, do you, even
though I've asked you into my house? You
don't think badly of me, do you? Young people
today are educated, they know how to see
these things in the right way, no? Love is always
beautiful, like a beautiful day, and it's always
proper if it's done right, no? (p. 215)

Lastly, the grandfather, 'a master so full of generosity'
(p. 109), who drives away the old woman who has
come to the house to blackmail his daughter-in-law
and pours scorn on provincial prejudices:

So, tell me this woman has a lover. Tell me who
it is, and how many times she's seen him. Well,
what do you think? That we would turn her
out for this? Or for one of your nasty ideas we
would damn her and punish her for ever? Get
out, get out while it's clear to go . . . and take
your heap of infamy with you. I can tell you
and all your town-full of hypocrites that she's

a poor woman who has fallen in love. She's
incapable of hiding anything, in what she does,
in how she acts—because she's honest, because
she's open, and because she's not like your race
of bigots and liars (pp. 110–11).

But faced with such sexual and political didacti-
cism, Damìn's black truth opens up like a gaping chasm,
with no prospect of redemption. Blinded by fear, prone
to sadism and self-destruction, the boy cannot understand the cobbler's words of advice, not even when they
become an urgent plea: 'Climb out of that vase or
yours, Damìn, it's time' (p. 86). In the end he will betray
the man who tries to be his teacher, fixing his sense of
guilt for ever.

4. The tragedy moves towards its climax and its epi-
logue, with a pace and a solemnity at times classical, at
times archaic, during the staging of the rural festa organized by the Fascist regime to promote Mussolini's
policy of national self-sufficiency: the 'Battle for Grain'.

This scene has been recognized by two major Italian
poets—Giovanni Giudici and Giovanni Raboni—as a
typical example of Volponi's association between highly
dramatic 'bodily' sequences and pictorial representation.
According to Giudici, the scene 'could be set on the
fiery arenas of a pre-Columbian sacrificial rite': the
'powerful system of timeless poetical metaphors' that

occupy it—genuine traps laid out for the 'lector humilis'—belie the novel's seemingly 'attractive' or 'appealing' structure.[2] Raboni, for his part, has argued that the 'obsessive metaphors' here are 'represented as though they were bodies that provide shade, tangible objects' that have the 'paradoxical realism of an old master painter'. Damìn's obsession is said to be represented in this way as though coming 'from another shore' with 'a sort of furious linguistic detachment'.[3]

The long final sequence of the village festa is one of the passages in which the visual quality of Volponi's writing is most evident. First, the detail of the billhook is immediately apparent, glinting in the light:

> Protruding from the corner of the stage, in front of the orchestra and the microphones, was a large billhook. Damìn took note of it, and it left him with a firm impression of coldness and sharpness: there at the ready, as though it was about to rise up and strike. Everything, the whole stage, seemed to be whirling beneath the light so as to draw his eye towards that blade and that handle. [. . .] Yet this object that lay there ready seemed to elude him, and he was struck not so much by its

2 Giovanni Giudici, 'Accadde a Fossombrone' [Once in Fossombrone], *L'Espresso*, 14 June 1981.

3 Giovanni Raboni, 'Un giavellotto nel cuore del fascismo' [A Javelin in the Heart of Fascism], *L'Unità*, 13 July 1981.

shape as by its resemblance, however uncertain and imprecise, to Marcacci's African dagger (pp. 260–1).

Similarly, with powerful spatial and visual effects, there is an alternation between the hallucinated viewpoint of Damìn who exaggerates and distorts the vulgar ways of the 'enormous crowd of dancers' (p. 266), and the detached and compassionate position of the narrator:

The farm girls stopped dancing and most threw themselves to the ground, letting their petticoats ride up to their underclothes beneath bright costumes, revival of a false tradition for the ostentation of virtues now wholly forgotten (p. 261).

The entire episode of the dance is interspersed with various close-ups, beneath the chiaroscuro of the moonlight, with moments of high drama, in a superb dramatic crescendo which yet is kept under control by the terrifyingly solemn and cadenced scenic direction.

Damìn's journey and his destiny in *The Javelin Thrower* might therefore be compared, for the period it represents and for the tragic formalization of its style, with the apocalypse of Emanuele, the protagonist in *Aracoeli* (1982), Elsa Morante's final novel of the same period, which tells a similar story (in the first person) of the loss of maternal affection and a no-less-savage degeneration of sexual emotion. It has to be asked why two major Italian novels, both written fairly late on, in the early 1980s, should deal with adolescent alienation against the background of Fascism: the return to this theme may be seen as stemming from some deep social and psychological need to understand and examine that period of history, and perhaps our own period, in a way that can be measured only with the specific means of good literature.

5. Volponi seems to prefer more compact narrative structures arranged into episodes of highly autobiographical impact, where the material of a personal story, however much transfigured, is offered 'visually' for the consideration and interpretation of the reader. He doesn't reveal any specific identification with his most memorable characters, such as Albino Saluggia in *Memoriale*, or Gerolamo Aspri in *Corporale*, yet when he tells a story in a form similar to that of a diary, as with Guido Corsalini in *La strada per Roma* (1991), or particularly with Damìn Possanza in *The Javelin Thrower*, the author's position becomes one of defensive detachment. Individual pain is objectified and historicized so that it can be used by readers as a 'commonplace' and as a therapeutic and introspective resource.

In short, the specific scenic and visual quality of Volponi's writing is probably designed to create screens on which to 'project' the most dramatic scenes, indeed 'spectacle', 'background', 'scene', 'representation', 'film', 'design', 'image' are key words in the novel. Volponi draws his greatest inspiration and specific stylistic and thematic ideas not only from Italian painting of the fifteenth and sixteenth centuries, as well as from modern painters from Mario Sironi to Carlo Carrà, but also from cinema—in this respect, an interesting comparison can be drawn between *The Javelin Thrower* and Louis Malle's film *Lacombe Lucien*.[4] There is, moreover, in the novel, a declaration by the narrative voice, of metaliterary form, that expresses this tendency to reutilize the visual arts. In Chapter XVI, Damìn seems to find a prospect of overcoming his personal anxieties by mastering his skills in drawing while studying at the Institute of Art in Urbino.

> Drawing allowed him still to look beyond himself, to endure reality and to understand and preserve it in a way that didn't place him in immediate and bitter conflict with his inner self.
>
> Drawing brought those objects, daily episodes and landscapes under his control, into

4 Caterina Volponi, in conversation with the writer of this afterword, recalled her father's enthusiasm, while working on *The Javelin Thrower*, when he watched Louis Malle's film of 1974, which has many parallels with the story of Damìn. This was one of the French director's most controversial films because of his interpretation of that period and the disturbing portrayal of an antihero. Lucien is a young French country boy who, in 1944, becomes a collaborator, falls in love with a young Jewish woman and is executed by the Resistance.

a conception of himself, in relation to those scenes and objects, that did not, through their usual obstacles and associations, produce new motives for pain, or at least no inducement towards its continual expansion. For this reason he thought of his drawings as real, as an end in themselves, just as substantial, for his hands and for his eyes, as food to be snatched and fought over (p. 244).

A similar distancing and cognitive function is served by the historical realism in the novel. The setting in Fascist Italy in the years leading up to the Second World War and, in particular, in the central Italian region of the Marche, is described with detailed mimetic and realistic emphasis, starting from the adolescent portrayal of Damìn during the early period of success by the Fascist regime in organizing the leisure time of the masses.

The Javelin Thrower, with its obsessive theme and its linear and 'engaging' story, offers the opportunity to penetrate the mystery of Volponi's 'corporal' and 'visionary' writing: in his novels, the image of the body, rather than representing the point of natural separation from history, always forms an undercurrent for social relations, a crossover point when it comes to accepted forms of behaviour, contradictory values, the personal cost of hiding behind a public mask. As well as giving expression to libidinal impulses, the body (especially in times of more rapid change) has something to do with the material reproduction of existence and with labour. The Oedipal theme, therefore, far from resolving itself in its terrible archetypes, is brought face to face with history: Fascism seems to bear the dual responsibility of favouring industrial short-sightedness and greed and of fomenting dysfunctional emotions, propagandizing the most grotesque phallic, athletic and warlike mythologies. And yet the enthusiasm of his father Dorino for the innovations of industry, Damìn's exotic and erotic fascination with comic strips and 'colonial' cinema, and even the fatal attraction of Norma, 'woman of the city', towards a leader of the Fascist revolution, testify how the nexus between town and country, between modernization and tradition, beyond any ideological consideration, is always represented in Volponi as a profoundly complex and contradictory process.

Even the most beautiful passages in *The Javelin Thrower* seem to confirm this dialectic between body and history concealed within the tragedy of its protagonist. The similarity between the figure of Norma and the city of Urbino, managed by the masterful use of light, exposes the ambiguous and conflictual nature of the author's Marche roots (and of all roots in general), a deep and constant theme throughout Volponi's writing:

In the golden light of sunset the city relaxed
inside its symmetry, serene and solemn in every
street and piazza. Damìn was struck by the
strong resemblance he found between each
building, its light and its beauty, and the face
and figure of his mother: the same demeanour
and the same calm breath of light and movement. His mother was as beautiful and noble as
Urbino, as that city brimming with age and history and yet open and alive. Here too tyrants
and potentates had passed; it too had been
invaded and conquered by rival powers. The
scenes and marks of their violence and destruction must still have been there—even though
the light bathed everything in the same beauty,
and remained, once the sun had set, as if it radiated from the very surfaces that it touched.
[. . .] The light grew whiter, as if to follow the
remorse that now re-emerged in Damìn's breast.
He tried to hold on to that whiteness so as not
to be swept away once more by the waves of his
truth: so that he could stop before reaching the
usual, inexorable storm of punitive and painful
associations (pp. 236–7).

Emanuele Zinato